The Big Crush

Emily Chase

SCHOLASTIC INC.

New York Toronto London Auckland Sydney Tokyo

ISBN 0–590–33249–X

Copyright © 1984 by Judith Sachs. All rights reserved. Published by Scholastic Inc.

12 11 10 9 8 7 6 5 4 3 2 1   11   4 5 6 7 8 9/8

Printed in the U. S. A.   06

8 THE GIRLS OF CANBY HALL 8

The Big Crush

8 THE GIRLS OF CANBY HALL 8

CHAPTER ONE

There was a new notice up on the bulletin board outside the housemother's apartment. Dana Morrison saw it first.

"Anyone who would like to discuss early admission to college, academic difficulties, or personal problems should make an appointment with Mr. Michael Frank, Ext. 37. All appointments will be kept confidential."

Dana read it three times before the message registered. She shook back her long, dark hair and frowned, a deep crease appearing between her clear, green eyes. Then, as if she couldn't remember two little numbers and a man's name, she took out her pocket notebook and wrote down the information.

She didn't use it, though. She dragged through the next three days feeling low, feeling ugly, feeling generally as though the

1

world was coming to an end. She *never* felt like this! She was a cheerful person — her mother and sister would swear to that — and was completely able to handle adversity at all times. The problem was, there was no adversity to handle. She simply couldn't put her finger on a thing that was wrong.

"Do you have that pattern number I asked you for?" her roommate, Shelley Hyde, asked her late one Friday evening.

Shelley was sitting on one of the three beds beside Casey Flint, their friend from down the hall. Casey claimed that, without Shelley's constant nagging, she'd never get her French homework done. Consequently, she showed up more and more frequently for the evening study hours in Room 407, which Dana and Shelley shared with Faith Thompson. At this moment, Shelley was explaining a particularly weird idiom to Casey. The two girls had sworn to get through the entire new list their teacher, Mr. Bernard, had given them that afternoon, but between translating and laughing, they tended to get sidetracked every few minutes. Dana was half-concentrating on a novel, and Faith was reluctantly doing some calisthenics.

"The pattern? Dana, hello, are you there?" Shelley shook her blonde head in dismay at her distracted friend.

"Huh?" Dana wondered if Shelley had spoken in another language. Why couldn't she seem to pay attention these days?

"When you went into town? Remember? I asked you to write down the pattern number of that skirt I wanted to make?" She turned and grunted at Casey. "I wouldn't have asked my mother to ship that sewing machine all the way from Iowa, if I wasn't going to use it, right? But how can I use it, if I'm stuck with a roommate who's lost in the stratosphere and can't remember a simple thing like a pattern number?"

"Leave her alone, girl," Faith muttered from her languid position on the floor. "She's in a fog. And I don't think it's love this time. Whatever it is, it looks terrible."

With a sigh, Faith started on her push-ups. Her long-boned, dark brown hands trembled with the exertion, and she gave up after only five. When her father, Officer Walter Thompson, was alive, he made a big thing out of doing thirty push-ups in a row every morning. Before he hit the streets of Washington, D.C., he told his daughter, he had to be prepared. Faith had never had much interest in fitness before, but recently, she'd decided that this was one thing she could do for her father. Since he'd been shot in the line of duty, Faith had tried hard to emulate the best things about him. The push-ups didn't seem *that* important, but you could never tell. Anyhow, she reluctantly acknowledged, they were good for her. Like spinach.

"I don't know why you have to make such a fuss," Dana grumbled, finally roused from her somber reverie. "I just wasn't listening. And I did get the pattern number, Shel. It's in my notebook — in my bag."

"I'll get it." Faith hauled herself up and staggered across the room to Dana's desk, which sat in the corner beside Faith's. "Anything to avoid another five push-ups." She flipped through the latest entries, then stopped suddenly with a snort of laughter. "What's this! Call Mr. Michael Frank, extension 37, to discuss personal problems. Are you kidding? Do we actually have a house shrink?"

Casey looked up from her French with a smirk on her face. "I've been to at least three shrinks." Casey joked a lot about being a "poor little rich girl." Her parents were art dealers and traveled a lot — almost all the time, as a matter of fact. All her life, Casey'd been shunted around to boarding schools, and it showed. She loved playing the bad girl, even though she wasn't, which made headmistresses despair of her ever reforming.

"Michael Frank is not a shrink," Dana said quickly, feeling a flush rising from her neck to the roots of her dark hair. "He's a guidance counselor."

The others looked at her curiously, and then, because it was a strict rule never to pry, they went back to what they were doing. Only Shelley felt there was something left unsaid, so she gave Dana's shoulder a playful push. "You want to talk about early admissions, I bet. Your grades are certainly good enough. And you want to tell this counselor you know we're going to kill you if you don't stick around for senior year. You want back-up from somebody in charge. I warn you, though, it won't work. We'll cream you."

With that, she walked to her bed and turned her back on Dana, pretending that everything was settled, and that nothing was wrong. The atmosphere in the room belied her cheery tone, though.

The next morning, she ran more than her daily two miles in the crisp November air, trying to clear her head of the anxiety that clung to her like a barnacle to a rock. She took the path through the park that led to the birch grove in front of Charles House, and then started down the wooded foot path through the maple grove that continued past the Canby property line. Her long legs, clad in hot pink sweat pants, covered ground quickly. The rest of her body went along for the ride, but it wasn't paying much attention. The consequence was that she tripped over a root she hadn't seen and went sprawling. Her right hand made contact with the rough ground and began to bleed. Suddenly she was crying, and she hated herself for it.

"All right, what is it? What's the matter?" she demanded of the leafless trees. "Let's just think about this a minute." She rubbed her hand, then licked at the trickle of blood that tasted as warm and salty as her tears.

"There has to be something bothering me, because I don't act like this for nothing. Now we've got several categories of possible ailments. We've got school, home life, social life, and the rest of life — that'll do for a start." She was still crying, although she made every effort to staunch the flow of tears.

"One, school. My grades haven't been so hot lately, despite what Shel says. Two, my father married Eve, and it gets to me. Eve isn't bad, but she's not my mother. He could have married *her* again." She sighed, and rubbed her nose. "All right, no, he couldn't. That was just my fantasy. And what's done is done.

"Three, social life. I broke up with Bret Harper, but he was a heartbreaker from the word go, and I should have known better than to get involved. Anyhow, that was a long time ago. But it still upsets me sometimes, I guess. I wish I could like Randy more, but you can't *make* something happen. He's sweet, and kind, but he's so different from me. I'm a wild and crazy New Yorker, and he's a staunch and stoic New Englander. Finally, everything else. I feel rotten — four. So rotten I can't really get excited about school, or choir, or anything. And what kind of a friend have I been to Shelley and Faith lately? I've been distracted and unhappy, and I'm becoming a generally unpleasant person, so I better stop it!"

She laughed aloud, and the sound rebounded around the wintry landscape. If that guidance counselor saw her now, sitting on the ground crying and talking to trees, he'd be sure she was bananas. The thing was, everything that was eating at her had been going on for some time — there was nothing terribly new about any of her problems.

"This must be what they call adolescent anxiety," she said with a laugh, dusting herself off and standing up.

She remembered the day, right after the divorce, when her mother had come home from work laden with the latest books on the topic and had ceremoniously deposited some on Dana's bed and some on her sister, Maggie's. She hadn't said a word, but the implication was that they needed help. Maggie was only twelve then, and it was really hard on her. Not that Dana was that much more sophisticated at fourteen, but what could books do for her? Dana had been certain then that she didn't need help.

But she knew now that there *was* something wrong with her, and it could get worse if she didn't take care of it. There would be nothing to it. She'd just call this Michael Frank, who was undoubtedly a balding, fat, forty-year-old who wore rumpled suits and stained ties, and she'd talk the whole thing out in one afternoon. She wouldn't be going to him for help, exactly, but she'd be getting her feelings out in the open. It wasn't that she couldn't talk to Faith and Shelley — that wasn't it at all. But a new person, with a fresh pair of ears, who didn't know anything about her might be just what she needed. She started back along the path, bound for the dorm, feeling considerably better and very determined.

Sunday was the first snow of the season. There wasn't much of it — just enough to dust the paths and buildings with a thin white frost — but it was sufficient excuse for most of the girls to goof off.

"Let's go into town," Shelley suggested, going to the window to look out at the white flakes. She parted the batik curtains that had been her first sewing project for Room 407. It had taken her days to do them by hand, which was why she'd petitioned her mother to ship the sewing machine from Iowa. She looked at the others for suggestions, but no one made any. "Let's skip the mystery meat for lunch and go get a pizza. Pizza's even better when you've trudged through all that snow to get it," she sighed.

"Silly, there's not enough of this stuff to trudge through," Dana objected. "I wouldn't mind missing lunch, though. Let's do it." It was the most enthusiastic she'd been in weeks. Somehow the decision to begin Monday morning with a call to the guidance counselor had changed her outlook.

Faith couldn't help but notice the difference in her roommate's attitude. "You're a weird one," she chuckled, sticking her short afro under the red wool beret her mother had recently sent her. Although the salary Faith's mother made as a social worker wasn't enough for big luxuries, she made sure that her Faith never wanted for anything important. "Yesterday we couldn't have convinced you to go on an all-expenses-paid trip to Paris. Today, you're up for anything. Dana, are you sure everything's okay?"

"Couldn't be better," Dana responded, reaching for her down parka and starting for the door. She led the way out of their room and wrote, "Out to Greenleaf, noon; back by four" in big letters on the form that hung on the door. As they started down the stairs, they saw that they weren't the only ones with this idea — a crowd had gathered in the front hall to put on their gloves and scarves before braving the cold. Pamela Young was among them. For some reason, seeing her changed Dana's mind. Pamela, the daughter of a movie star, thought the world turned on her every whim. Her snobby, self-congratulatory attitude was something that Dana just wasn't up for, particularly in her current funk.

"You two go on without me," she said suddenly, watching Pamela tucking her perfect, shining blonde hair under a mauve cashmere cap.

"Dana?" Faith looked at her quizzically.

"It's just . . . I remembered something I really have to do. Go ahead, have fun. When you get back, we'll all go to song night together."

"Promise?" Shelley asked. She looked at Dana hard.

"Yes, of course." She shrugged off her parka as the others tramped out the big wooden front door of Baker House. A whistling, chill wind blew right inside, making Dana feel even colder, and more alone.

"I know why you're not going," Faith clucked, "and girl, it's a dumb reason. You don't even have to talk to that one." She jerked her head in Pamela's direction.

"Please come with us," Shelley begged, never being one to take an emotional no for an answer.

"I just really . . . I don't feel like it. See you later." Dana turned on her heel and nearly ran up the stairs, furious with herself for being cheery and on top of things one moment and depressed the next.

She reached the top of the staircase, panting and close to tears, and nearly knocked over Alison Cavanaugh, the housemother. The young, attractive woman grabbed Dana by the shoulders to prevent being butted in the stomach, and laughed as she pushed her large, hornrimmed glasses up on her nose. Alison was the person everyone turned to in a crisis — her understanding, good humor, and quick appraisal of situations was legend — but somehow, Dana didn't even want to look at her today.

"Hey, you, what is this, football practice?" Alison grinned.

"No. Sorry, I wasn't looking," Dana muttered.

Alison's eyes flickered, as they always did when she was sizing up potential trouble. "Everyone's gone to Greenleaf to frolic in the snow," she commented. "Whats'a matter, not up for frolicking?" she teased gently.

"I think I'm getting a cold," Dana lied. "I was just going to my room."

"Come to mine instead. I'll make us some tea and put some Vitamin C in yours. Let me play mommy."

The word almost wrenched a sob from Dana, who was struggling to keep herself under control. "Not now, Alison," she said as she pulled away and took off for her room. As she closed the door behind her, she couldn't remember when she'd ever felt so miserable.

CHAPTER TWO

The voice Dana heard on the telephone was low and understated, like the rumble of distant thunder. He didn't sound young or old, or really very interesting. She could hear a pencil scratching on a pad as he wrote down her name and the time — 4 PM on Monday.

"Is that convenient for you?" he asked politely.

"Ah, sure, yeah. I mean, yes, that'll be fine," Dana had stammered nervously. Nothing seemed fine, but it was the kind of thing you said to an adult.

"I'm the third one down the row in the East Faculty houses. You'll know it because it's the only one with a red bike parked outside. I hope you don't mind meeting me there — my office isn't really set up yet."

"That's fine. Ah, see you then. Bye."

"Bye, Dana."

He rode a bike — that meant he couldn't

be *really* old. Although some old people rode bikes. There were some practically ancient people who went tooling around Central Park while Dana jogged, back home in New York. Maybe Michael Frank rode a bike because his doctor had told him it was good for his heart, at his age.

"Oh, this is ridiculous," she muttered to herself as she left the phone bank on the main floor of Baker. She was already late for her third period class in Main Building, so a few minutes more wouldn't matter. Anyway, she hadn't read *Twelfth Night*, which Mrs. MacPherson had assigned over two weeks ago. This was terrible, Dana thought to herself as she crossed the snow-dusted campus. She was always the first one to raise her hand in English, but today. . . .

"Mind if I walk with you?" A voice interrupted her reverie.

"Oh, no. I mean, be my guest," Dana said, recovering her poise. It was Pamela Young — just her luck!

"I just loathe this weather, don't you?" Pamela said with disgust, wrinkling her delicate nose. She was wearing a cape with a real fur collar, and she looked just about as theatrical as her movie-star mother. The cape was nice, Dana conceded, but it was perfectly ridiculous for a Monday afternoon on Canby Hall campus. "Back in California, we *never* have to worry about the cold," Pamela went on. "Can you believe it — I had to get a *whole* new wardrobe, just to come East!" She laughed, a brittle little tinkle, like a crystal dinner bell.

Dana just grunted and walked a little faster. She couldn't imagine why Pamela wanted to walk with her, and she had nothing to say to her anyway.

"Where are your Siamese triplets?" Pamela asked. "I thought you three never went anywhere without each other. Sometimes it looks like you're attached at the hip."

Dana stopped in her tracks, turning to the other girl with a look of disgust on her face. Pamela had tried once to break up her friendship with Faith and Shelley, and though she hadn't been successful, Pamela had a spiteful streak in her that just wouldn't stop. "Pamela," she said evenly, "I have some serious thinking to do right now. If you don't mind, I'm not really in the mood for a conversation."

"Well, of course. Don't bite my head off, dear. I was only asking an innocent question." She shrugged, then marched off quickly in front of Dana, who hung back watching Pamela purposefully stride ahead in her brand new cordovan leather boots. It was dumb, letting Pamela get to her. The girl was plain mean, and everyone knew it. Every word that came out of her mouth had a barb attached to it — even the ones that sounded perfectly nice. The best thing to do was to stay out of Pamela's path.

Dana put on some speed as she glanced down at her watch. There was nothing she could do now — the choice was skip class entirely or walk in unprepared and late and have everybody stare at her. "Might as well take my lumps," Dana muttered as she entered Main Building.

Mrs. MacPherson scarcely glanced at her as she slid into her seat. The teacher, a former actress, had just launched into her own, rather Wagnerian rendition of Viola's speech that began, "Make me a willow cabin at your gate," and she was oblivious to the world, or at least to the class.

"What happened to you?" Shelley hissed as Dana hurriedly opened her notebook. Faith looked at them across the room with concern.

"I had to make a phone call," Dana explained.

"Oh, *that* call," Shelley said knowingly.

"What are you talking about?" Dana was immediately on guard.

"Young ladies!" Mrs. MacPherson couldn't exactly ignore the undercurrent of whispers that collided with her own rounded tones. "I'm terribly sorry to disturb you, but this is Shakespeare. And no matter what you're discussing, I'll warrant that *his* words are better than yours."

"Sorry," Dana mumbled, praying that she wouldn't be called on. If she could just make it through this period, she knew she could last till four o'clock. So she put her head in her book, tried to look studious and intelligent, and held her breath. It worked. There were some times when thinking invisible made you invisible.

Dana took the path through the woods that she usually jogged along when she wanted peace and silence. As she approached the faculty houses, she was certain that this mission would be a successful one. The quiet was almost deafening — everyone else was at some afternoon activity or at the library. Maybe he'd forgotten and wouldn't be there; maybe she'd freeze and wouldn't have a thing to say. Although she'd tried to prepare her thoughts on her way over, her mind was suddenly a blank, and her palms felt clammy inside her thick wool gloves. Maybe this wasn't such a hot idea after all. Maybe she should just turn around and go back to the room and have a Tab and do some homework.

But then she saw the red bike, the paint chipped and worn. It looked homey and comfortable and made her feel that maybe its owner would be the same. She stepped up to the door of the small brick building with its white trim and hesitated just a moment. She'd never been inside one of the faculty houses, and just being here was slightly intimidating.

Go ahead, get it over with, she thought

desperately. Then, closing her eyes, she put her hand on the brass knocker and rapped sharply on the door.

Silence. Nobody home?

She was about to turn away when she heard a voice — the same low rumble she'd heard over the phone earlier in the day. "C'mon in, door's open. Don't trip over the boxes!" he called out.

She turned the handle and walked inside, skirting the haphazardly stacked cartons that were everywhere — in the hall, on the stairway, in the next room. As she stood there, wondering what to do, a man appeared at the top of the stairs, carrying another box.

"Hi," he smiled. "I see you found me."

He wasn't old and fat and balding at all. In fact, he looked something like the Marlboro man, rugged and devastatingly handsome. He was only about thirty, Dana judged, with dark, almost black, curly hair, worn a little long in back, and rich brown eyes, underscored with laugh lines. He was wearing old, faded jeans, a black turtleneck sweater, a red-and-black plaid lumber jacket, and sweat-socks. What Dana really liked about him was that he wasn't plastic-handsome — his features were kind of irregular — but the way they all fit together was really something. He got to the bottom of the stairs and extended his hand to her. He was just about her height.

"Hi," she said, and swallowed hard.

"I'm sorry for all the mess," Michael Frank told her, gesturing around the hallway. "You can ask anybody — my mother, my sister, even — and they'll tell you I'm a terribly neat person. But moving! It's the worst! Every time I move I swear it's the last, and here I am, doing it again. Let's go in the kitchen — I could use a Coke, how about you?"

She was too dumbfounded to speak, or even to ask why he'd just moved in, so late in the term. It probably wasn't any of her business, but of course, she was curious. She followed him into the small, sunny kitchen and took a seat at the old wooden table, as he put down the box carefully and took two cans of soda out of the refrigerator. But she didn't have to ask. He answered her as though she had spoken.

"I should have been here a month ago, but my last employer refused to let me go. Miss Allardyce, as you can imagine, was not pleased.

"This is your second year here, huh?" Mr. Frank switched the focus to Dana so quickly, she didn't have time to be astounded that he'd bothered to find out anything about her before meeting her. "Oh, sorry," he smiled, a dazzling, beautiful smile, "I didn't offer you a glass. I always drink out of the can myself."

"I never use a glass for Coke either," Dana said easily, waving him away from the box he had hurriedly begun to scrounge through. "Now ginger ale, though, that's a different story."

"That drink has real class," he agreed. "Class deserves a glass."

They both laughed.

"How about some corn chips to go with that?" he suggested, opening the cupboard that was completely empty but for the single bag of chips. "I know this junk can kill, but I'm addicted."

"Me, too," Dana confessed, digging her hand into the bag as he sat down and offered it to her. They both munched for a moment unself-consciously.

Then they sat there, on either side of the table, just staring at each other. "Yes," Dana said at last. "To answer your question, yes, it *is* my second year. What'd you do, get out the file on me?"

"Uh-huh. I can tell you your whole life story. But I won't bore you," he grinned, tipping far back in his chair. "Do you like it here?"

The question was so innocuous, Dana didn't even wonder why he'd asked. "Well, yes. Most of the time, it's great." She was hesitant about being critical in any way. After all, she didn't think it was Canby Hall's fault that she felt so down.

"When I was at school getting my master's in psych," Mr. Frank said, "I kept thinking I was too old to be cracking books. I mean, all my friends were working, earning money, and there I was in Berkeley, getting another degree. But I couldn't deny I liked school. School was . . . satisfying. You took tests, you got grades, and sometimes you learned something." He leaned back even further and took a sip of his Coke as though he really enjoyed it.

"You're from California?" Dana asked, forgetting it was Mr. Frank who was supposed to be asking her the questions.

"Chicago. I just went out West for my master's. And for a city boy like me, all this Massachusetts countryside is a little overwhelming. It'll be nice for jogging, though — a real break from pounding the cement pavements."

"I jog, too, Mr. Frank," Dana offered, feeling an instant kinship with this man. She was a city slicker, just like him.

"Oh, please don't call me that," he exclaimed in mock horror. "It makes me feel so old. How about Michael?"

"Okay," she agreed.

"You know, the best place I ever ran was New Mexico. I was working on a Navaho Indian reservation one summer."

Dana felt the weight of so many days roll off her, and suddenly, she wanted to confide everything in this extraordinary person. But she didn't feel rushed — the confessions could wait. "What were you doing with the Indians?"

"Learning about them and how their society functions. I was also recovering from a short marriage."

"Oh." Michael Frank was divorced! It didn't seem possible. What woman in her right mind would ever let him go?

He got up and crossed the room, eyeing the stack of boxes suspiciously. "Why don't you postpone my odious chore of unpacking a little longer and tell me what's eating you. I mean, I'd be perfectly happy just to swap life stories, but you sounded pretty low on the telephone. Do you know what's the matter?" he asked.

"Frankly, no, I don't." She paused. "I guess it's a lot of things."

"Your folks are divorced, aren't they?"

"Uh-huh. But so are the parents of about half the kids here. No, I stand corrected — probably 75%. It's an epidemic!"

"Pretty gruesome to be a statistic, isn't it?" He went over to the sink and leaned against it, crossing his muscular legs.

"Oh, I don't mind that so much. I mean, I don't care about how many people have to go through this. It's just what it means to me. That sounds kind of selfish, doesn't it?"

Michael shook his head. "Not to me. Remember, it's you who has to live your life. All the different pieces of it add up to making you happy or sad. Or something in between. You can change most of what you don't like yourself — but what your parents do just happens to you."

"That's true." She looked up at him, realizing for the first time that the worst things that occurred were those she had no control over. Like her father's new wife. "I know divorce is supposed to be sad and marriage happy, but it was just as hard to go to my father's wedding last June as it was to watch him move out of our apartment," she said slowly.

"Do I detect an evil stepmother lurking in the wings?"

"Eve's not evil," Dana protested.

"Well, good." He breathed a sigh of relief. "I'm delighted to hear she's not *that* bad."

"No, not at all." Dana fingered the rim of her Coke can. "I kind of like her, in a way. She's not my mother, of course, but I suppose she'll make my father a better wife than my mom did. He didn't really want a career woman, and when the advertising agency he works for moved him to Hawaii for a year last June, Eve just stopped working to go with him. My mom would *never* have done that."

"Do you think this family stuff has kind of warped every other part of your life? I don't know," he added quickly. "I'm just wondering."

"I don't think so. I mean, most of my life is just terrific. I have the best roommates in the world — Shelley and Faith — who'd do anything for me. We really love each other. And I do well in school most of the time, if I concentrate. Everything's good!" She said the words loudly, as though she were trying to convince herself they were true. Then she frowned. "So what's wrong?"

He chuckled and shook his head. "I'm a guidance counselor, Dana, not a crystal-ball reader. Let's see . . . how about boys?"

"Well, I have a boyfriend — I mean, a good friend who's a boy. Randy. Nothing special. I went out pretty steadily with some-one last year, but that's ancient history." She didn't want to discuss Bret with Michael. As she sat there really talking to this fascinating man and marveling at the way he really listened to her, she couldn't believe that she'd ever been interested in someone as shallow and superficial as Bret.

"Okay, you don't sound like a terminal case to me," Michael said, starting on the top box, which was filled with mismatched plates. "But maybe we should get together again next Monday — same time, same sta-tion. Over the week, you can think about some of the things that really tick you off. Little things — maybe they'll seem incon-sequential to you, but write them down any-way, for my benefit. And I promise, the place will be immaculate the next time you come."

She got up and came around to the other side of the table. "I like it this way," she offered.

"Oh, you're just saying that to make me feel better. Now you have to get out of here. I can't bring myself to unpack if there's somebody around to talk to."

She nodded and started for the door. Then she turned back. "Is this . . . um, your office?" she asked.

"No — Ms. Allardyce has given me the conference room in the Main Building. Once my secretary, Jane, and I get it set up for seeing students, it'll be fine. But right now, it's the pits. Much too stark and institutional. You know what I mean? It's not homey — you can't sit on the floor and kick off your shoes. So until I get a few pillows scattered around and remove the vinyl chairs, I'm using my house instead."

"I think that's a very good idea," Dana told him. "Well, thanks. See you in a week."

"I'll see you before that," he promised. "I'm always around. It's been nice meeting you, Dana," he said, and he meant it.

She left him to his boxes, and on her way out, she turned once to look around. This was where he lived, where he would settle in and make his home. At least, she hoped he would. She closed the door softly behind her, feeling better than she had in months. Michael was clearly an exceptional person — maybe the most exceptional man she'd ever met. He was wise and mature and he had a way of putting things that made them seem sensible and even comprehensible.

Also, he seemed to know what she was going to say before she said it. That was uncanny! And whatever had passed between them during the last hour, it was obviously the beginning of a very fine friendship.

Dana walked down the steps of his house, surprised to realize that, despite all her good feelings, she was still a little depressed. All right, problems, like pimples, didn't clear up overnight — she knew that. At least she had some hope, now, that eventually she would feel better.

Dana touched Michael's red bike like a talisman, a promise of things to come.

CHAPTER THREE

W ell, where *is* she?" Faith took her tray off the salad bar and scouted out a table near one of the windows that flanked an entire wall of the dining hall. Shelley followed her, scrutinizing the strange meal she had assembled for herself. In the past months, she'd dropped most of the fifteen pounds that had clung to her chunky frame since childhood. Having shed her unwanted flab, she had no intention of gaining it back again. Thus, dinner was cottage cheese, green salad without dressing, and a small slab of the main course, which the cook euphemistically called "roast beef with natural gravy." Whatever RB with NG really was, the girls had decided, it sure wasn't natural.

"I don't know. I haven't seen Dana since English. Oh, there's Casey!" Shelley waved across the hall at their friend, who made a beeline for their table.

"How'd it go?" Casey asked. "What's the counselor like?"

"We don't know. Neither of us have seen Dana," Faith said. She watched her roommate push a piece of salad around her plate as though it were a hockey puck. "Shelley, are you going to eat that stuff, or do we bring it up to Doby as a treat?" Doby was Alison's calico cat, an illegal resident of Baker House. "And where's the dessert? You know you can't think straight without your sugar fix."

"Not any more," Shelley said with grave determination shining in her blue eyes. "I'm giving it up. You know Alison says that sugar and junk food are the cause of all the violent crime in the United States today," she joked, picking at the dry meat.

"Listen." Casey unloaded her piled-up tray, which was groaning with an unusual selection of salads, hot vegetable dishes, and three pieces of pie. "We've all agreed you look great thinner, Shel, but let's not carry this thing to an extreme. You're going to have to sew yourself a whole new spring wardrobe if you keep going at this rate."

"And I'll give *you* all my fat clothes." Shelley looked at her friend's full tray with fascination.

"Hey, there's Dana. Dana, over here!" Faith yelled.

Dana, who'd been standing right behind Pamela Young on the serving line, trying to look preoccupied so she could avoid another conversation, looked up with relief as she heard Faith's voice.

"Be right there," she nodded, grabbing a glass of milk and the roast beef. She couldn't help wondering what Michael Frank would be eating for dinner. Did he cook for himself in his kitchen, or would he eat in the faculty dining room?

"Well, she looks all right." Casey smiled indulgently as Dana took a seat beside her at the oak table. "He didn't have the usual effect on you, then."

"What's that?" Dana asked curiously.

"Oh, he didn't change your brain wave patterns, or like that," she grinned.

"No, of course he didn't." Dana sighed and started on her food, which looked even less appealing than usual tonight. She didn't really want to talk about her session with Michael. It was something very personal, very precious.

"Well, what happened? Do you feel better?" Faith asked. She assumed that a guidance counselor would, like her mother the social worker, have the ability to change bad for good, to make a difference. Although it was true that, for many of her mother's poorest clients in Washington's ghetto, there wasn't a whole lot she could do. "I don't know, girl, you look pretty far away right now," she commented when Dana was silent.

"You're not supposed to talk about what happens with your shrink," Casey explained. "It's confidential."

"At least tell us what he's like," Shelley persisted. The reason she was particularly interested in Michael Frank was that something had been bothering her lately, although she didn't want to talk about it with her friends. She'd figured that if Dana had some success with this guidance counselor, she might just make an appointment with him herself.

"He's . . . very nice," Dana said in a guarded tone. It was almost as if she would give away something of her own by describing him.

"Here, Mary Beth. There's room at this table." Pamela Young led the way across the dining hall toward them, and Casey gave a moan of desperation as she saw the three newcomers.

"Why? Why us?" she grunted, sliding her tray over to make space for Ellie Bolton and Mary Beth Grover, who'd recently been hanging around with Pamela. Neither girl really seemed to enjoy Pamela's company, but Pamela had latched onto them. The movie star's daughter had changed her clothes for dinner, as was her custom, and tonight she was dressed in a trim beige silk knit dress with burgundy piping at the neck and sleeves. Dana had to admit that she looked perfectly gorgeous.

"It gets so crowded in here at 6:30," Pamela was saying as she sat down next to Shelley. "Although with the food they serve, I can't really understand why."

"I love it," Casey said, just to be contrary. "I could eat this food till the cows come home."

Pamela gave her a withering look. Ellie, a tall, self-possessed junior with wheat-colored hair, took a sip of her tea and directed her gaze at Pamela. "Well, go on," she said. "Tell us more about him."

"Have you seen the new guidance counselor?" Mary Beth asked the others before Pamela could answer. "I mean, he is to die from!"

"Have you?" Dana asked quickly. She hated the idea of sharing Michael with these girls.

"No, but Pamela says —"

"He's really something. Definitely Hollywood quality," Pamela cut in knowingly. "I hear he's only thirty or thereabouts, and unattached. When I was living at home, lots of my friends were dating older men," she added.

"Boy, is that dumb," Faith chuckled. "I mean, what could you possibly have in common with someone that old?"

"Oh, my dear," Pamela said patronizingly, "older men bring so much experience to a relationship. But naturally, when you're not ready for that, it doesn't mean anything.

Now, I haven't *actually* talked to him, but if
his personality comes anywhere close to his
looks, I'm certainly interested."

"Dana's talked to him," Shelley boasted.
"She spent an hour with him today."

"Is that true?" Mary Beth's ivory com-
plexion flushed bright pink. "Really, Dana?"

Dana felt an uncontrollable urge to escape.
This was ludicrous! What's more, it was unfair to Michael. "If you'll all excuse me," she
said hastily, grabbing her tray and pushing
away from the table, "I have to get to work.
I've got a history paper due Thursday, and I
haven't even started it."

With that, she was gone, not feeling the
slightest pang about leaving her friends
alone with horrible Pamela. They were perfectly capable of getting out of her way if
they wanted to. And as far as Dana was
concerned, if Faith, Shelley, and Casey
wanted to gossip about this new "Hollywood
quality" person, as Pamela insisted on putting it, then they deserved anything she
dished out.

Shelley approached the faculty house with
enormous trepidation. In Pine Bluff, Iowa,
when you grew up in a nice, solid drug-
gist's household, you didn't go to outsiders
for help with your problems. If her brothers,
Jeff and Larry, could see her now, they would
undoubtedly scratch their heads and chuckle.
Their little Slugger, as both boys called her,

on her way to talk turkey with a psychologist! And what would Paul say! Shelley had gone steady with Paul up until the day she left for Canby Hall, and she loved him dearly. Of course, she loved Tom Stevenson, too, but that was different. Tom would probably understand, because he was heavily involved as an actor in the Canby theatrical productions, and he would appreciate the fact that an actress had to watch her figure.

And that was the problem, in a nutshell. As Shelley had begun to lose weight, she realized that her attitude toward food had changed. And it worried her. There were so many awful stories these days about anorectic girls who kept themselves at starvation levels, refusing to eat for fear of gaining an ounce. They thought they were fat even when they weighed under a hundred pounds! If there was any possibility that Shelley was developing anorexia, she wanted professional help, and she wanted it immediately, before the problem got any worse.

"Hello? Anybody home?" she called as she pushed open the door.

"You must be Shelley. Hi, I'm Jane, Michael's secretary." The young woman welcomed Shelley into the hallway, and took her hat and coat, which she placed on the antique oak hat rack that stood by the door. At that moment, Michael Frank came down the stairs, calling his hello. At once, Shelley understood what Pamela meant. Michael was, in fact, as gorgeous as she'd said he was. But she could also see why Dana had been so annoyed. Michael didn't look like the kind of person you should judge in an instant, and even though he was extraordinarily handsome, there was clearly more to him than his good looks.

"Thanks, Jane," Michael smiled. "We'll be in the parlor if you need us. But no phone calls."

"Yes, sir! When you two are finished, would you help me move some of those boxes of files over to your office? My arms are about to fall off."

"No problem. Leave them for an hour and catch up on your reading," Michael suggested.

The woman saluted, then left them alone.

"Um, I'm sorry to bother you," Shelley began as he led her into his very neat sitting room, which faced the maple groves. The late afternoon sunlight made a striped pattern on the old-fashioned horsehair sofa with funny, carved mahogany legs.

"What do you think Ms. Allardyce hired me for?" Michael smiled, his keen eyes appraising Shelley closely. "Aren't you Dana Morrison's roommate?" he asked.

"One of them, yes. Faith Thompson's the other one."

"I understand you three are really close buddies. That's rare in a boarding school, you know. So often, there's lots of competition between the girls, lots of bad feelings."

"Not with us," Shelley said at once. "We're crazy about one another. Sometimes, we're just crazy."

Michael laughed. "That's why I took this job. I have to confess I'm a little crazy myself."

"Oh, good!" Shelley settled back on the sofa, looking across at Michael who sat on the floor with his legs crossed, tailor-fashion. "Dana needs to talk to somebody," she added. "She's been awfully low lately."

"What about you?" Michael was all too well aware that many kids, rather than talk about their own problems, would prefer to dig around for information about their friends' troubles. His rule was strict — no divulging of anything that had occurred between him and another student.

"I'm okay," Shelley said quickly. "The thing is, unlike my roommates, I have an out when I'm feeling blue. See, my passion is the theater. It's wonderful, when you're really miserable, to get up on a stage and be somebody else for a while. You know what I mean?"

"Right. I acted in college a little. I was terrible, though."

"I'm not bad. Getting better." She stopped, unable to think of any way to bring up the dreaded topic. Now that she was sitting here, it seemed kind of stupid. "I really love the classics. Tom — he's a friend of mine at

Greenleaf High and an actor himself — he taught me how to appreciate great literature."

Michael kept his mouth shut, waiting. Eventually, when she trusted him enough, she'd tell him what was on her mind.

"I come from the Midwest," Shelley went on, talking a little too fast because she was nervous, "and in Iowa, people just don't do things like they do in the East. If my family knew I was here . . ." she laughed.

"Well, they never will know," Michael said seriously. "So don't worry about that. It won't go on your permanent record, either."

"Oh." Shelley felt something loosen up inside when he said that. "That's good. Well, I guess you want me to put up or shut up, right?"

He shrugged. "Say whatever you'd like, Shelley. You can even tell me I have bad breath, if you want."

She was totally amazed. He just didn't talk like a teacher — or even like Alison. "It's my eating habits," she blurted out. "I'm a little worried about them."

"You like pickles and ice cream?" he asked cautiously.

"What?! Oh, no, Mr. Frank, not *that!*" She couldn't believe he'd said it, but he had. "No, you see, when I came to school last year, I was, well, overweight. That was nothing new — I'd always been . . . let's call it 'pleasingly plump.' Naturally, when I was fat, there was nothing pleasing about it. Anyhow, I lost weight this term, and I was proud of what I'd accomplished. Only now, I have this funny feeling that I may gain it all back. So I . . . this is going to sound absurd —"

"Go ahead," he prompted, listening intently.

"I'm scared of eating. But I'm also scared of that disease I've heard about."

"You mean, anorexia?"

"Uh-huh. Do you think there's any chance that I may be heading for disaster?" she asked earnestly.

"Well. . . ." He got up off the floor and walked over to the window, his rugged face accentuated by the beam of light that streamed across the room. "Let me ask you a few questions. When you look in the mirror these days, what do you think?"

Shelley grinned. "I'm astounded. I really look much better thin."

"You don't still feel fat?"

"Not at all. I feel normal."

"That's great. It shows," he smiled, turning to her. "How do you feel about a chocolate ice cream soda smothered with whipped cream?"

"I'd give it up in a second for a whole batch of my mom's peanut butter cookies with chocolate kisses melted on top. Those are my absolute favorite," she grinned.

Michael's eyes lit up. "You think you could get her to send us some? Just for scientific experimentation, of course. And to satisfy my own ravenous craving. My grandmother used to make those when I was a kid back in Chicago. I would have killed for those cookies."

"Really? I'll write her tonight," Shelley offered. "She used to send cartons of them on a regular basis — until I asked her to stop. But if you'd like some, by all means!"

"Only if you promise to share them with me." Michael walked over and stood in front of her, the laugh lines deep now under his deep brown eyes. "I don't think you're in any danger of starving yourself to death, Shelley. The girls who do that have very severe problems about their own self-images — they can't see themselves as attractive, no matter what they do, or how thin they get." His kind face was warm and understanding, and Shelley found herself relaxing suddenly. She was very happy she'd come.

"What do I do about being scared, though? Every once in a while, somebody offers me something to eat and I panic. It's totally ridiculous, but I can't seem to stop it."

Michael scratched his head. "Do you have a scale in the dorm?"

"There's one in the locker room at the pool," Shelley told him.

"Well, get yourself down there every day and stand on it. If you're maintaining your weight, you'll see for yourself that everything you put into your mouth isn't going to affect the way you look. Pretty soon, you won't be so scared of those cookies. How about it?"

"That's a brilliant idea," Shelley exclaimed, getting up and going to the door. "Why didn't I think of that?"

"You would have, in time," Michael assured her. "I'm just here to speed up the process."

"Thanks," Shelley sighed, reaching out to shake his hand. "I didn't think I could talk to anyone about this — least of all a man — but it turned out to be pretty easy, after all."

"I'm glad. See you around, Shelley." He led her to the front door where she took her things off the hat rack and quickly dressed to go out into the chilly day.

"Bye," she waved, walking out the door and down the steps. She was smiling when she got back to the dorm, and she was also very hungry.

She raced up the stairs of Baker House to Room 407, where Faith and Dana were going through a stack of Faith's photographs, the ones she'd taken in town the day of the snow. Faith was the most active photographer on the Canby *Clarion*, the school paper, and everyone agreed that she was incredibly talented. Her dream was to be a top news photographer for a big paper by the time she was twenty-five.

"I like this one best," Dana said, picking up a shot of two little boys, sitting on the steps of Greenleaf's Town Hall, pelting each other with snowballs. "What do you think, Shelley?"

"Michael is *wonderful!*" Shelley exclaimed, tossing her coat and hat on her bed. "Oh, guys, I feel terrific."

Faith shook her head. "You're pretty mysterious. I didn't even know you had an appointment with the guidance counselor."

"No," Shelley said, slightly embarrassed to be keeping things from her roommates. "I didn't think my problem was important enough to complain about. And guess what — it's not."

The other two looked at each other, and for a moment, Dana felt something akin to jealousy. Of course, that was nonsense. Everyone at school might be going to see Michael to discuss one thing or another, for all Dana knew. After all, he'd been hired to take care of everyone, if they needed him.

"Well, I can't be the odd man out," Faith shrugged, picking up the next batch of photos to flip through. "Guess I'll have to dream up something to talk to him about." She smiled mischievously. "Too bad I'm such a cheery kid, huh?"

"No, it's not." Dana pulled herself out of her fog and threw an arm around Faith, hugging her tightly. "If you weren't on an even keel, all of us would fall apart." It did puzzle her, though. Of the three of them, Shelley was the last one she would have suspected as needing a counselor. But then again, it was none of her business why anybody else would feel the need to talk to Michael.

"Phone call for you, Dana!" Heather, the dorm monitor yelled as she rapped on the door. "Sounds real long distance."

"Thanks. Be right there." She jumped up, hoping against hope that it might be her father, calling from Hawaii. She glanced at her watch. It would have to be very early in the morning there, she thought as she raced down the stairs to the phone bank.

"Hello?" She was breathless as she picked up the receiver.

"Hi, sweetheart. It's us!" John Morrison's loving voice crackled over the long-distance wires. It was hard to believe, as Dana stood here in the phone booth in her dorm in Massachusetts, that her father was nearly 6,000 miles away in Honolulu.

"Dad! How are you?"

"Great. Really wonderful. And you?"

She wouldn't burden him with her mixed feelings. "Pretty good. What's up, Dad?"

"Eve and I are flying in for a long weekend next month. I know you get booked up in advance, so I wanted to reserve you for the thirteenth and fourteenth. How's that? We'll be staying at the Westbury since we sublet our place. We'll either get you a room there, or you can stay with your mother and Maggie, as you like."

"Dad, why would I stay in a hotel in New

York?" Dana asked unbelievingly. Ever since her father had remarried, he'd gotten some pretty weird ideas. "I mean, I *live* there."

"Sure, baby. We just thought it would be fun for you. But you do what you want. Can't wait to see you. We have some marvelous news."

"Oh, what?" Suddenly, Dana had a funny feeling in the pit of her stomach. She'd already been through the crunch three times — first the divorce, then her father's wedding, and finally, his moving all the way to Hawaii. Could things get even more messed up?

"Can't tell you now. You'll have to wait. You always loved surprises, right?"

"I used to," she said sullenly.

"Good. So just hold your horses. Eve sends her love, sweetie. See you next month."

"Bye, Dad." As she hung up, she felt deflated, like an old, tired balloon. She didn't want any surprises. All she wanted, she suddenly realized, was to see Michael.

CHAPTER FOUR

On Sunday evening, right after dinner, Dana found a note in her mailbox. She noticed it only because it was the sole slip of paper in any of the boxes in Baker's front hall.

"Dana," it read. "How about a run tomorrow? Meet me at my house at four, ready to go. Michael."

She was both thrilled and anxious. If she could, she would have started out for Michael's right away and gone for a moonlight jog. It seemed an eternity since last Monday, and she had so much stored up inside her, so much to tell him. She tucked the note in her jeans pocket and slowly walked up the stairs to Room 407.

Faith was hoisting one eight-pound weight in each hand as Dana entered the room, which had been torn asunder to accommodate the new "gym," as Shelley called it. Faith had moved all the furniture around

so that she could put her mats down on the
floor, and the result was utter chaos. The
three girls had long ago decided that they
needed a homey atmosphere in order to survive, and what they had now was far from
the look they'd worked so hard to create. In
their first weeks at school, they'd put their
bed frames in the storage room so that they
could sleep on mattresses on the floor, which
they piled high with their quilts and blankets.
Right now, all three beds lay in a row, almost on top of one another.

Luckily, Faith had done nothing to the
posters and photographs they'd hung up to
cover the walls they had painted black in a
rash moment, but any day, Shelley was certain, there would be body-builders where
once there'd been Humphrey Bogart and the
Joffrey Ballet. Shelley was very worried about
her dried flower arrangement on the win-
dowsill, too. In a fit of muscular energy,
Faith was bound to knock it over and take
Shelley's piggy bank with it. As Dana walked
into the room, Shelley was eyeing Faith's
strenuous activities with extreme skepticism.

"Shel, guess what?" Faith grunted and
put down her weights. "I've decided to do
my laundry. Want to come and do yours,
too?" Faith collapsed in a heap on the floor,
her cut-off gray t-shirt soaked with perspira-
tion.

"Hi, guys." Dana walked past her exhausted
roommate and went to her desk, where she

promptly filed Michael's note in her top drawer, under a letter from her father.

"What about you, Dana? Want to come along?" Faith asked, hauling herself up and wiping her face with the towel from around her neck. She raised her two weights high, then dropped them on the floor with a bang.

"Maybe I will," Dana said quietly, unable to get into the spirit. She couldn't remember when she'd last done her laundry. Probably not for weeks, the way she'd been feeling. And her hot-pink sweat pants were really grungy. She couldn't look terrible tomorrow.

"I can't believe it," Faith chuckled, gathering underwear and socks from the bottom of her closet. "There are trolls living down here! Incredible."

Shelley was sitting at her sewing machine, a frown creasing her forehead as she puzzled over two pattern parts for her new skirt. "I'd come with you, but I have to get this done. Tom said he'd stop by and take me for a quick spin at eight. You do understand, don't you?" She put her foot down on the treadle and sewed a seam, then screamed, and dropped the material as if it were hot. With a sigh, she started in with the seam-ripper.

"The way you're going, girl, you might as well ask Tom to run the thing up on that motorcycle of his." Faith winked knowingly at Shelley.

"Very funny. Now get out of here, please, and let me concentrate."

Faith and Dana bundled up their clothes and put them in the plastic hamper, which Faith lugged out the door as Dana followed with detergent and fabric softener. She hated doing laundry, but it was a good escape from doing anything else.

They made their way down the stairs, past the lower hall where Baker girls were lined up three deep at the bank of telephones, waiting for the chance to call home. Sunday nights were the worst as far as homesickness was concerned, and the sound of a parent's voice was very important to most of them. Pamela Young was monopolizing one of the phones, chatting on as though she were in her own bedroom at home. It was indicative of everyone else's attitude toward Pamela that no one was waiting behind her. They knew better.

Faith and Dana walked down to the basement, past the game room, where two freshmen who didn't know better were playing ping-pong. Real Canby Hall old-timers avoided ping-pong like the plague, claiming it was the most un-chic activity available. Only dolts played it. Faith gave the two misguided girls a meaningful look, which neither of them understood. Then she dug deep into the pocket of her sweatpants and pulled out one lone quarter. "Did you bring

our piggy bank?" she asked as she squan-
dered her last cent on a bag of peanuts from
the candy machines that Alison kept stocked
with health food. The bag of nuts rolled out
on its metal tray, and Faith grabbed at it as
though she hadn't seen food in a year. "This
is all I've got with me," she sighed as she
led the way into the laundry room at the end
of the corridor. "I don't think the washing
machine accepts nuts."

"Oh, no, how stupid of me!" Dana felt like
kicking herself. "I forgot the money. I'll go
back."

"Never mind," said a voice from the depths
of the laundry room. "I'll spring for a few
loads of wash if you'll keep me company."
It was Alison, and she certainly did look
glad to see them. Her wild mass of reddish-
brown hair had been hastily tied in a pony
tail at the nape of her neck, and her glasses,
as usual, seemed to be about to catapult off
her nose. "I think laundry should be abol-
ished as a national pastime, don't you?" She
jumped up and jiggled her change purse at
them.

"I'll vote for that," Faith giggled. "You
know, this is really depressing."

"What do you mean?" Alison asked, following the girls over to two vacant washing
machines. The steady hum of the dryers was
oddly soothing in this stark room of pipes
and overhead hanging lightbulbs.

"I mean, *you're* still doing this and you're

a grown-up. We have nothing to look forward to!" Faith complained, dumping half the contents of the hamper into one machine.

"My mother sends everything out," Dana commented. "But she works full-time and more, so she says she's entitled. And the longer she works as a buyer for that prestigious department store," she added with a grin, "the more laundry she manages to accumulate."

"Someday," Alison clucked, feeding quarters into Faith's machine, "I'm going to make enough money so that I never have to do laundry again."

At four o'clock the next afternoon, Dana was waiting eagerly in front of Michael's house, jogging from foot to foot to stay warmed up. She had a ribbon in her hair today, just for a change, instead of the sweat band she always wore. As she rang the doorbell of the faculty house, she couldn't help but feel excited. After all, how many girls did Michael Frank go running with?

Jane answered the door and smiled as she glanced down at the hopping girl. "I thought about taking up jogging once," she said with a cynical smile. "So I laid down until the thought went away."

Before Dana could respond, Michael was at the door. He bopped his secretary playfully on the head. "That's an old one, Jane. All the flabby people who need an excuse have a line like that. Whereas Dana and I —" he paused, and leaped athletically down the three steps of the house, "— we can go out and do our miles and not feel guilty about having ice cream for dessert."

"Who's guilty?" Jane asked, patting her rather ample hips. "I enjoy my vices. Have fun, you two." Shaking her head, she closed the door on them.

"Where do you usually go?" Michael asked, leaning down to stretch his palms to the frozen ground. Dana liked his outfit — he was wearing navy blue shorts over his gray sweatpants and a hooded red sweatshirt with the faded black letters, "BERKELEY" on the back.

"Through the maple groves, then around onto the road that fronts the property, then back toward the dorms," she told him. "There's usually not too much traffic."

"It's not more than three miles round trip, is it?" he asked anxiously, getting down on the ground to do some bent-knee sit-ups. "I turn into a pumpkin after two and a half."

"No," Dana smiled. "I'm not good for much more than two myself." This was a lie — lately she'd been doing more — but she didn't want to show him up. She wanted, in a way, to be just like him, to share his short-comings as well as his successes. She got down beside him, maybe five feet away, and did some sit-ups of her own.

"Have a good week?" Michael asked as they both got up and leaned from side to side to get the kinks out of their waists. "I've been so busy getting my office set up, I haven't really had time to circulate."

Dana was glad of that. She had this unreasonable fear that everyone in Canby Hall would have a better reason to see Michael than she did. Of course, if she were really, seriously depressed, she'd have a good excuse for seeing him on a regular basis for the rest of the semester. Not that she wanted to feel bad, but it would be better to feel awful and get to talk to Michael about it, than not feel anything at all.

"I guess," she commented while bending over and swinging her torso from side to side. "Are you warmed up yet?" She wanted to sprint away with him, to run by his side and never stop.

"I'll never be ready," he laughed. "Let's go." He let her lead down the path at a slow, easy pace and stepped into line beside her. Their feet crunched steadily on the rock-hard earth, and they could see their breaths coming in great puffs, like cartoon-strip balloons, above their heads.

"The one thing that really strikes me about Canby Hall," Michael said without breaking pace, "is how terrible the food in the dining hall is. How do you girls handle it?" He wasn't even breathing hard.

"We keep a supply in our rooms," Dana explained. "Of course, much as we try to persuade her, Alison won't go for hot plates. She's always claiming we'd set the place on fire, and I guess there really is some town statute about it. But we've got tuna and peanut butter and lots of soda. Occasionally we go into town to the pizza place, and if the weather's really bad, we've got the salad bar in the cafeteria. But you're right, it's pretty ghastly," she panted, trying not to sound like she was working too hard.

"Alison?" Michael asked. "That's Alison Cavanaugh?"

"Right — housemother. I mean, that's kind of a funny thing to call Alison — when you see her you'll understand what I mean. But she keeps the dorm running smoothly, and if we ever have problems, we can go up to her apartment and discuss them."

He glanced at her curiously, his deep brown eyes trying to read her expression. "So why didn't you go to her when you wanted to talk?"

"Oh, well, she's really somebody you go to with minor problems; you know, like when Faith and Shelley and I weren't getting along, or when Bret was acting really awful. He's the guy I used to go out with. Problems like that."

"I see." He was silent, waiting her out. For

a few minutes, there was no sound in the deep woods other than that of the slap of their feet on the dry ground.

"Anyhow," Dana said at last, "she knows me too well."

"What do you mean by that?"

"You know. Familiarity breeds contempt."

He paced a little faster as he turned away from her. "Don't be coy with me, Dana. I asked you a straight question."

She looked at him, puzzled by his sharp answer. "I didn't want to tell Alison — or my roommates. I didn't think any of them could understand. But you. . . ." She shrugged and stopped running.

Michael stopped, too, and Dana stood beside him and looked at the ground. There was a pool of ice with one leaf frozen into it. To Dana, it looked like a heart, perfectly still, frozen in time. "I did what you told me to. I wrote down all the things that bothered me during the week."

"Good. Hey, can we run? I'm stiffening up."

She nodded and they started off, but now their steps were out of synch. Dana didn't try to match his paces — just to think of what she had to say. "There's Faith and Shelley's attitude toward me, for one. It's like I've suddenly become fragile, like they're tiptoeing around me. But," she added, "it's possible that I encourage that. I guess I haven't been myself lately."

"Maybe you should mention it to them the next time you see them," Michael suggested.

"I suppose. My father called," she blurted out. "From Hawaii."

"Yes? Did you tell me he was going to be there for a year?"

"Till next summer, if all goes well. I mean, his ad agency just sent him to straighten things up out there. They didn't say anything about his staying permanently." She said this to reassure herself. Somehow, she wondered if her father's "terrific news" might have something to do with a permanent appointment to the fiftieth state. "I guess his wife's okay. They're coming to New York next month for a long weekend, so I'll see them then."

"How do you feel about that?" he asked, his eyes peering straight ahead, out into the distance. They were on the town road now, and the paved ground made running easier. They picked up some speed.

"I don't like it," she said, answering truthfully for the first time. "I mean, can you imagine, he actually asked if I wanted to stay at a hotel with them. In New York, where I *live*, for heaven's sake!" She snorted with annoyance at the thought.

"Did you tell him you wouldn't do it?"

"Of course. My mother and Maggie — that's my sister — wouldn't dream of my not staying at the apartment when I'm in

town. It's my home. It's always been home."
As she said the word, an image formed in
her mind of the way it used to be, before
her father moved out.

As if he knew what she was thinking,
Michael asked, "How old were you when your
parents split?"

"Fourteen. Maggie was two years younger.
I remember the day — it was so weird. We'd
gone shopping with Mom, and when we got
back, Dad was sitting in the living room,
not reading or anything, just sitting there. I
thought it was odd — lately he'd been getting home late after dinner every night. He
and Mom never fought, really; they were
just terribly silent sometimes. Anyhow, he
was sitting on the couch and not in his favorite chair, and I thought that was peculiar,
too. We all came in, laughing, and dropped
our packages. Then he said, 'Would you girls
come here for a minute? Your mother and I
have something to tell you.' Mom's face
turned gray — you know what I mean, not
white but deathly gray — and she said, 'Not
now, John.' But he insisted. They'd apparently been planning it for a while, and he
decided he couldn't hold out any longer.
Whew!"

"What did you do?" Michael's voice was
soft.

"I didn't cry, but Maggie did — she
wouldn't stop. I kind of got very tight and
still, and I stayed that way for weeks. I

practiced smiling in the mirror, as if I'd forgotten how. But I don't think I cried about it until a month after he was gone. Well, he wasn't actually gone — he got an apartment right across town — but he wasn't home. He'd never be home again." She sighed as a stiff wind came up suddenly and carried her words away. "And that's it — the tragedy in twenty-five words or less."

"Don't be flippant, Dana. Not with me."

She was so grateful he'd said that. It was as if she could pretend with everyone else in the world, but with Michael, she would have to strip away all the pretense. "Okay," she agreed.

They turned and started back toward Canby Hall just as it started getting dark. For a while, they ran together effortlessly, despite the cold and the wind. It was funny, Dana thought, but talking about really big things while she ran made it easier. Michael had probably suggested this on purpose, thinking that if she was sitting in his office or his kitchen, she'd be careful about what she said. He was so smart about things like this.

Together, they slowed their pace and trotted down the path that led to the dorms. Their hour was over.

"Well, it's been . . ." Dana began. Then, to her dismay, she saw the figure sitting on the steps of Baker House. He was wearing his down parka, and his dark blond hair and high, etched cheekbones were unmistakable, even at this distance. It was Randy Crowell, the Greenleaf boy Dana had been dating off and on since she'd broken up with Bret Harper. She hadn't talked to him in a week. As he saw her coming toward him, he stood up and waved. "Dana!" he yelled. "Over here!"

"Someone to see you," Michael commented. "I better start back to my house."

"Oh, no, that's all right. I mean . . ." Dana stammered. She didn't want her time with Michael to end.

"Come by my office next week, if you like. It'll be set up by then. Bye, Dana, thanks for the run," he said, and sped off.

"You know, I've been looking for you everywhere," Randy said as he approached her. His gray eyes were clear and piercing, and they showed how much he'd missed her.

"I was just out jogging," she said, suddenly feeling guilty that she'd neglected him. Of course, he hadn't called her, either. It wasn't all her fault.

"How about a movie this weekend?" he asked.

"I don't think so, Randy," she said hastily, feeling the chill of the air now that she wasn't moving. "I've got an incredible load of work. Maybe some other time."

"As you like," he said, clearly disappointed. "Well, you better get inside before you freeze up. See you, Dana."

"Bye, thanks for stopping over," she said lamely. She put her hand on the doorknob and was about to turn it when he called back to her. "Hey, is Canby Hall having their annual midwinter dance?" he asked. "And can I wangle an invitation?"

She turned and smiled, flattered by his interest. He really was a great-looking guy — not rugged enough to be called handsome, but more ethereal; poetic, even. "Sure, I guess. I hadn't thought much about it. You're welcome to come." That sounded awful! "I mean, I'd be really delighted if you'd take me."

"It's a date, then." His face beamed with pleasure. "But maybe we can see each other before."

"Give me a call," she suggested, knowing already that she would have too much to do whenever he asked her out. He just didn't seem a . . . a priority. She waved good-bye and went inside. The oak-paneled lounge was warm and cozy, girls sitting around sprawled on the overstuffed sofas and armchairs or lolling around the Oriental rug that covered most of the large room. They were all faintly illuminated by the antique brass lamps that were always kept polished to a brilliant gleam. A delicate glimmer of light still remaining in the sky shone through the leaded-glass windows, touching the nearest girls with a rosy glow. Dana looked at them all and suddenly felt older, more mature. Michael understood that — nobody else really knew her, but he did.

With a firmer step, she went up to Room 407 to shower and change. There was nothing terribly wrong with her, she decided, but she certainly had a lot to discover about her feelings.

CHAPTER FIVE

Faith and Casey peered down the long stacks of books and then at the title on their library slip. "I can't believe I'm supposed to read a book called *Huguenots At The Brink*," Faith muttered.

"What are *hewgwenauts*? Are they like astronauts?" Casey asked.

"Idiot! The Huguenots were French Protestants from the sixteenth century. I mean, they did something important to change the course of French history. I think," she added.

"Sounds like heavy dozing material," Casey said decisively. "If I were you," she smiled, "I'd pick out a nice romance or photography book or something and tell the history teacher that someone else absconded with his precious hugo-whatevers. Just say they were lined up in the aisles three deep for it, and you got there too late."

"Let's see." Faith kept going, ignoring

Casey's persistent chatter. "The number's 677.25 — that should be over here."

"I feel the book's magnetic attraction already, drawing us closer," Casey snickered.

"Okay, 677 . . . here it is!" She plucked the tome off the shelf.

"Just your luck — a fat one. Books with titles like that never come under five hundred pages."

She grimaced as Faith reluctantly stuck the book under her arm and started walking toward the library tables, which were jammed with students anxiously preparing for midterms.

"There's no room for us to sit down," Casey hissed.

"Too bad this book circulates," Faith sighed. "I guess I have to take it out."

"Why don't you conveniently misplace your library card?" Casey suggested helpfully.

"I'll have to read it sooner or later," Faith said, gritting her teeth. "History marches on."

"Would you two mind keeping it down?" Pamela Young's strident whisper came from the closest seat. "Some of us are attempting to absorb some knowledge."

"Right, like the paper towel you really are," Casey whispered under her breath. Faith doubled over, clamping a hand over her mouth. She really hated making noise in the library. From the time she first began to read,

her mother had drummed into her the notion that silence in the library, as in church,
was more than golden. It was *mandatory*.

"C'mon, let's get out of here," she suggested quietly, dragging Casey away before
she could make another rude remark. The
next one would undoubtedly be worse, because Casey's wit improved once she got
rolling. They ran, giggling, to the front desk,
where Mary Beth Grover was seated, glumly
filing library cards.

"You want to check this out?" she asked
as Faith slid the book in front of her.

"No, I don't. But I don't have a choice."

Mary Beth shrugged and stamped the
book, then Faith's card. "Enjoy," she smiled
as the girls picked up their things and walked
past.

They wandered down the corridor toward
the front door of the library building. But as
they passed the conference room, they
couldn't help noticing the man who was
down on his knees near the windows, arranging a battery of large pillows on the floor.
The room had been emptied of all furniture
except for a couple of file cabinets and a
chair, and it looked much larger, very inviting.

"Hello." Casey pulled Faith through the
open door. She smiled as the man turned on
his haunches to greet them, and then she
gasped, thrusting out her elbow to give Faith
a sharp poke in the ribs as she suddenly

realized who he was. Shelley had mentioned that the guidance counselor's office was in the library conference room. "Oh, hi!" she went on before he could respond. "Aren't you Michael . . . uh, Mr. Frank?"

"You were right the first time," he nodded, coming over to them. "And you are — ?"

"Casey Flint and Faith Thompson," Casey grinned, walking past him into the room. "Looks like you're setting up shop."

Faith hung back by the door, just listening. She was always a little wary of people in authority when she first met them.

"What do you think of it?" Michael asked, surveying his quarters with the two girls.

"Not bad," Casey told him.

"It looks real cozy," Faith said. "Well, nice meeting you, Mr. Frank. I have work to do, unfortunately," she added pointedly to Casey, who sighed and nodded.

"See you." He smiled in an appealing, friendly way.

As the girls started out the door, they were surprised to see Alison bearing down on them, her arms loaded with books. She was moving so fast, in her usual near-run pace, that she didn't look where she was going and tripped. The books went flying.

"Just my luck. And I'm late, too," she grumbled as they all bent down to help her. "I completely forgot that these are two weeks overdue. And on top of that, Ms. Allardyce is waiting for me. What a day! Mercury must be in retrograde," she sighed. Then she grinned like a guilty schoolgirl. "Hi, Michael," she said.

"How are you? Haven't seen you in a while."

Faith and Casey looked at each other. "Do you two know each other?" Casey asked curiously. They certainly looked as though they did.

"We're still in the acquaintance stage," Michael said. "Let's see, there were the three faculty meetings, and the fire drill at the faculty houses, and then there was the time Alison spilled her cup of tea all over my hand in the faculty dining room."

"I did no such thing!" Alison exclaimed, pushing her wayward glasses back up on her nose. Her face was a bright pink.

"You did. At least it was cold tea." Michael laughed, and the two girls joined in.

"I think it was because I was eating a large sugar doughnut," Michael said, his brown eyes never leaving Alison's. "She looked at that thing as though she wanted to kill it. Your housemother's a health nut, in case you haven't noticed."

"How could we help it!" Casey shrieked. "Listen," she added in an undertone. "We've got a great stash of candy bars back at the dorm. If you're ever desperate. . . ."

"Thanks, Casey, I'll remember that." Michael gathered the books from the girls and took the one Alison was holding. "You better not be late. I'll return these for you," he told her.

"But I — well, that's awfully nice of you," Alison acknowledged. Faith could never remember seeing her look so flustered. It was as if he'd asked her on a date instead of offering to return her library books.

"Now run," Michael urged her. "I'll see you later."

Without a word, Alison sped down the corridor and out the front door of the library building. Faith watched Michael, who had a rather smug, self-satisfied look on his face.

"We've got to go, too," Casey said hurriedly, plucking Faith's sleeve. They followed Alison out the door, into the damp afternoon air that smelled of distant chimney smoke and wet leaves.

"What do you think of that?" Casey muttered.

"You mean, the two of them?"

"Well, it makes sense," Casey said, slowing her walk to a stroll. She always walked slowly when she thought out loud. "They're two attractive people, stuck here in this bleak desert of a girls' school, and when you think about it, there's really no competition for either of them. Look, can you imagine Alison with Mr. Bernard? Or Michael with Ms. MacPherson? Nooo way! I think these two will make a good couple," she finished as they walked up the steps of Baker.

"Hold on, for heaven's sake. He *said* they

were just acquaintances," Faith pointed out.

"Girl, did they *look* like acquaintances?"

"Well. . . ." Faith thought about it for a moment, then shook her head.

"If there isn't something going on between those two, then I'm a . . . a Huguenot!"

"Finally — you got it!" Faith laughed. The girls linked arms and walked inside the dorm, savoring the warmth of the front hall. They sped up the stairs to Room 407 and burst inside. Dana was sitting across the room from Shelley, quizzing her on her French idioms.

" 'A little later,' " she read from the grammar book.

"*Toute suite?*" Shelley asked hopefully.

"Wrong," Casey chimed in. "Put the books down, you two. Wait till you hear the news!"

"What's going on?" Shelley asked, gladly ceasing work on her most unfavorite subject.

"It's the new guidance counselor — you'll never guess whose library books he offered to return — if you get my meaning," she added slyly.

"What are you talking about, Casey?" Dana was immediately uncomfortable. Why was everyone always prying into Michael's private affairs?

"It's Alison," Faith continued. "I mean, it looks like they're getting pretty tight."

"It wasn't just the books," Casey interrupted excitedly. "It was the way they were with one another. Oh, you know, Dana! Remember back to the way you used to be with Bret — only older."

"Casey, you are constantly jumping to conclusions, are you aware of that?" Dana asked sharply. Suddenly, she had an intense desire to dig herself a little hole and crawl inside it. She wished she could turn her mind off, and her ears, so that she wouldn't have to hear what Casey and Faith were saying. It didn't matter that it wasn't true; it was merely the fact that they were gossiping about him.

"Are you guys really certain about this?" Shelley asked, sliding off the mattress to sit on the floor. "This isn't the kind of thing you should start rumors about. Unless, of course, they aren't rumors."

"We don't have any proof," Faith acknowledged, pulling the beret off her short afro. "It's just a feeling. So I guess this information shouldn't go outside this room, just to be on the safe side. But it sure did look like sparks were flying between them."

"I think you're both ridiculous." Dana stood up in a huff and strode to the door. "How can you make up a romance based on seeing two people having a discussion about . . . what was it? Library books."

"There's the words that people actually say, Dana," Casey said slowly, as if explaining it to a child, "and then there's the subtext —

what goes on underneath. If you'd been there, you would have seen it, too. It was unmistakable."

"What was? Answer me that," Dana demanded. "You have such a vivid imagination, Casey. You'd probably think that Michael Frank came to this school for the sole purpose of meeting a woman, like it was some stupid dating place. Just because he's unmarried and smart —"

"And gorgeous," Casey prompted.

"I'm glad," Dana clenched her teeth, feeling hot tears rushing to her eyes that she refused to let out, "that I don't judge people by physical standards. You and Pamela Young seem to feel that the only important thing is what a person looks like. I think that's pretty sad."

"How can you compare me to Pamela! Dana, she's a crocodile!" Casey looked genuinely upset.

"I'm sorry." Dana swallowed hard, choking back the sobs. "That was hitting below the belt. But I still think you shouldn't talk about him. All of you." She turned on her roommates. "I would hope you three could find something more valuable to do with your time than gossip."

She walked stolidly to her closet and pulled her running clothes from their hook. She'd already done her miles that morning, but she couldn't stay in the room a moment longer, and she didn't know what else to do. Without a word, she tucked her things under her arm and walked out, making a beeline for the bathroom down the hall. The others just stared at the door she'd slammed behind her.

"What's with her?" Casey demanded.

Faith sighed and looked at Shelley. "Are you thinking what I'm thinking?" she asked quietly.

"It sure looks like something we've seen before." She turned to Casey. "Dana has a first-class crush. I honestly didn't realize it until just now."

"Oh, no," Casey wailed, sitting heavily on Dana's bed. "You know what this could do to her, don't you? I mean, Bret Harper was a real louse, and he enjoyed adding notches to his belt whenever he could. In my opinion, the bum hardly counted as a human being, so she was able to get over him. This guy is something else. You know, he's like a real man, a real person. Like somebody you'd want your older sister to marry. It's going to hurt terribly."

Shelley's face was suddenly white and distraught, as though she felt her friend's pain in her own gut. "What can we do? We've got to do something."

Faith shook her head. "This isn't something we can fix, Shel. Dana's going to have to suffer her own way out of it. The really sticky part isn't Michael, though — it's Alison. Or, it's Michael and Alison together.

That's what's going to hurt worst of all."

The three girls sat there in silence for a long time, thinking about Dana's situation. Casey thought that having parents she hardly ever saw was awful, but that experience had toughened her for the rest of life. Faith thought about the day she and her mother and brother and sister got the terrible phone call from the precinct, saying that her father had died. If she could survive that, she knew she could take anything that would come her way in the future. As for Shelley, she thought briefly that of all the girls, she was pretty lucky. Her parents loved each other and were together. And she'd managed to stay in love with Paul back home in Iowa and still have a wonderful time with Tom right here in Greenleaf. Someday, she might have to make a decision, but certainly not now.

They all thought about Dana, then. They knew how bad her parents' divorce had been for her, but the fact remained that she still had a father and mother who loved her. She'd once said that breaking up with a guy, having loved and then moved on, might be an interesting experience. Dana pretended to be cool, unaffected, to be able to handle any amount of adversity. But when it came right down to it, they all decided, Dana was the last person who would be capable of getting over a crush on an older man. She was just too vulnerable.

"Well," Casey said at last, getting up and going to the door. "I just hope it's not a battle to the death between her and Alison with grizzly headlines in the local paper like 'Coed Kills Housemother In Love Nest.'"

"Don't joke about it, Casey," Shelley barked. "It's not funny."

"Not only isn't it funny," Faith agreed, "it's downright bad for the morale of the dorm. Listen, you two, we have to keep this news under our hats just as much as the stuff about Michael and Alison. Maybe Dana will get over it when she sees she's outclassed."

"Or maybe," Shelley said sadly, "her heart really will break this time."

The three girls were so absorbed in their own thoughts, they didn't even bother to answer the door. Someone had been knocking persistently for the past two minutes, but none of them seemed to hear. At this moment, nothing mattered to any of them except Dana.

CHAPTER
SIX

"Well, who *is* it? Keep your shirt on!" Casey stormed to the door and flung it open, feeling nothing but annoyance. Who could be so insensitive at a time like this, when Dana's romantic entanglement hung suspended in air? Only someone who didn't understand the meaning of closed dorm doors.

"Hi, where's Dana?" The visitor was Pamela Young. Casey gave her a look of disdain.

"I really wouldn't know."

"She went out to run, Pamela," Shelley offered. As much as she disliked Pamela, she saw no reason to act like her and be purposely rude. "She's either in the bathroom getting dressed or outside warming up. But I really think she'd like to be alone right now."

"Thanks," Pamela offered breathlessly, already on her way down the hall. As she reached the bathroom door, she pushed it open, looking around the white-tiled room for signs of life. "Hello, anybody here?" Her voice echoed and bounced off the walls.

Dana was standing in front of one of the five sinks, splashing cold water on her flushed face. At the sound of Pamela's voice, she didn't even bother to turn around.

"Oh, am I glad I found you!" Pamela came over and peered at Dana through the mirror. Clearly, Dana thought, it was just so she could check out her own impeccable appearance.

"I'm on my way out to jog, Pamela."

"But this is a life-and-death matter. Really," she added, putting one beautifully manicured hand on Dana's wrist. "You're the only one who can help me."

Dana sighed and sucked on her lower lip. This was the last thing she needed right now! But she was a sucker for being told that she was invaluable — when her sister Maggie pulled it on her at home, she always gave in eventually. It just seemed strange that of all people, Dana would be the one Pamela would pick. She always thought Pamela was above sharing her problems. Dana had a perverse desire to know what was eating the other girl.

"Okay," she said at last. "But I can only spare a few minutes right now."

"I'll be brief," Pamela promised. "It's my grades. I'm in lousy shape."

"Why don't you ask someone to tutor you?

There are plenty of seniors who do it all the time."

"That wouldn't help. That'd just be a Band-Aid on the gushing wound." Pamela slumped against one of the sinks, and Dana had to steel herself against feeling sorry for her.

"You think you're going to fail a midterm, right? And get docked from the midwinter dance? Well, it would be bad, but it wouldn't be the end of the world." She paused, considering her words. "Maybe if you buckled down and studied a little more. . . ." It was a well-known fact that Pamela claimed she could look at a textbook once and memorize the page, because she had a photographic memory. Faith's comment on first hearing that was that you had to put film in the camera before you could take the photograph.

"Listen, Dana. It's too complicated to explain, but you've got to trust me, just this once."

Why should I? You've always been a sneak and a liar, Dana thought to herself. Aloud she said, "What do you want from *me*?"

"You're seeing the guidance counselor on a regular basis, aren't you," Pamela said rather than asked. "I mean, it's none of my business, but people have seen you at his office and out on the road, running with him. You two must be pretty tight."

Dana tightened her lips, thinking that this was exactly what Faith had just said about Michael and Alison.

The Big Crush 73

"I wouldn't say that."

"Look, Dana, if you could just talk to him for me, sort of put in a good word before I go see him. I got an official message that I'm supposed to appear promptly at noon tomorrow, or else. I think it's about . . ." she hesitated, then decided to spill the whole story, ". . . about my flunking out. I'm really scared."

Dana wondered if this was all an act. But why would Pamela bother making up a story for her benefit? She did look distressed, so much less in control than she usually did. If Ms. Allardyce was actually going to expel her, she had cause to be upset. There was a rumor going around that her movie-star mother had sent her to Canby Hall to straighten her out, because she'd already been asked to leave one boarding school. It really would look terrible on her record if she was forced out of a second.

"Pamela," Dana began slowly. "I'm sorry, but I don't see what I could do. Or why I should do anything for you. Michael Frank is a very fair person as far as I can tell, and I'm sure he wouldn't recommend tossing you out of school before he'd given you a chance to get your grades up. He's not an ogre or anything."

"I know I've treated you terribly. And Faith, too. But please, would you just tell him I'm trying? See, he has the last word in cases like this. The teachers can report to Miss A. that I have bad grades, but only he can tell her if I have the motivation to change. So, if you could manage to fit it into the conversation somehow that I really *want* to get better. . . . Please, Dana."

"We don't talk about other kids, Pamela. We just stick to the subject of . . . of whatever I came to talk about. I couldn't just suddenly bring you up." She was still puzzled. Pamela had such a roundabout way of airing her problems that it was difficult to believe her, no matter how serious she sounded. Dana couldn't just forget how she'd tried to break up her friendship with Shelley and Faith.

"Please, just say you'll mention my name. I know you have more influence on him than anybody — I mean, it's obvious, isn't it? A faculty member wouldn't go jogging and stuff with a student unless their relationship was very special."

Dana couldn't help but feel that Pamela was right. After all, Michael treated her, not like a client, but like a friend.

Pamela's eyes were soft now, and she looked so vulnerable it was hard to hate her. "Just — tell him I'm not a rat, okay?" She was pleading now, actually reduced to needing Dana.

"All right. All right. Now, can I go run, please?" Dana asked.

"Of course, and look, I really appreciate this. Any time you need a favor, or want to borrow some of my clothes or something, just ask."

Dana nodded, hurrying out the bathroom door with a sense of relief. She hoped Michael would be impressed by her kindness if she talked to him about Pamela. She was a little bit ashamed to realize that she had an ulterior motive for being nice to Pamela. And yet, she thought as she bent down to warm up, it couldn't hurt.

In the next two weeks, she saw Michael a lot. Not that she was depressed. Actually, she felt a lot better, but she always found that she had something to tell him or show him, or she'd happen to bump into him as he was starting off on his run and they'd naturally go together. That was the great thing about their relationship — it was natural, it felt easy.

She did manage to mention Pamela, but got no reaction. If Michael had any opinions about the other girl, he didn't let on. Pamela had been sullen and nasty ever since her first interview with Michael. Everyone just assumed, when she didn't show off any new dress for the midwinter dance, that she wasn't going. She said nothing else to Dana about her predicament, much to Dana's relief.

Then there was the matter of Randy. He'd called frequently, and she'd always found some excuse to cut their conversations short. As for going out with him, it was unthinkable right now. She'd be with him at the dance, and it would probably be nice to see him, in a way, but she had too much on her mind to clutter it up with more emotional baggage. Their friendship was coming to a head — she could see it — but she didn't want to deal with it. Michael was the most important person in her life now.

She and Faith and Shelley had done really well on midterms, which was amazing, considering how far behind Dana had been just before Michael had come to Canby Hall. She was back on top, getting practically straight A's, and although they weren't as important to her as they had been in the old days, when all she had to think about was grades and roommates and boyfriends, they were certainly nice to have.

"I can feel spring in the air," Faith sighed as the three of them sat on the front steps of Baker one Saturday afternoon, the week before the dance. "Can't you smell it?"

"That's the Greenleaf dump, dear," Shelley offered, raising an eyebrow at her friend. "They're burning trash again. You must really have spring fever if you think it smells good."

Dana listened to the two of them with one ear, a dreamy smile on her face.

"What are you wearing to the ball, Cinderella?" Faith asked Dana, poking her lightly to get her attention. She was aware that she'd been acting extra nice to Dana these days, ever since the business with Alison, and sometimes it felt a bit awkward. They used to be so close they could say anything to each other.

"I guess my dress jeans and that wild blouse Eve sent me from Hawaii. And my cowboy boots," Dana said. "What about you?"

"Oh, it doesn't matter what *I* put on." Faith chuckled as she laced her dark brown fingers in back of her neck and gazed up at the sky. "Johnny loves me for myself." She grinned at the other two. "It's not what's on the outside that counts, it's my moral fiber he'll be looking at."

"Sure he will," Dana smiled. "What are you wearing, Shel?"

Shelley frowned and shook her head. "Nothing fits me. I don't know. . . . Maybe if I was just a bit thinner, I could wear some of your terrific-cut slacks," she sighed. "None of my old things look right," she finished decisively. Despite her talk with Michael and her frequent trips to the gym locker room to stand on the scale, she still worried about her weight. Worried far too much. She hadn't mentioned it to anyone, but her goal was to lose three more pounds by the time the dance rolled around.

"I'll lend you anything you want, Shel," Dana said magnanimously. "We'll find something wonderful."

The girls smiled at each other, and for a moment, the old feelings of complete and total fight-to-the-death friendship surfaced once again. They were still smiling when they heard the sound of Alison's old VW Beetle pull into the drive beside Baker. Dana looked up anxiously, and the other two girls exchanged glances. Dana had been pointedly avoiding Alison lately, and Shelley and Faith knew exactly why.

"Well, hello you three." Alison grinned brightly at them as she started up the walk. "Isn't it a bit chilly for prolonged exposure?"

"We were just going in," Dana said, getting up and propelling herself toward the door.

"Alison! Your hair!" Shelley exclaimed. "You had it cut!"

"The word is *styled*, Shelley." Alison patted the neat waves that just brushed the collar of her coat. Then she did a little pirouette so they could see the back. "I went all the way to Cambridge for it so it better be good. What do you think? Honestly, now."

"It's great," Faith declared, coming over to give it a closer inspection. "I mean, it's different but it's still you. Nothing drastic." Alison's wild reddish-brown mane had been layered skillfully and tamed. Dana stood at the door to the dorm, her hand on the knob. If she didn't turn around, she wouldn't have to see how super Alison looked.

"Well, run inside and put on your glasses so you can examine the results," Shelley urged, taking her housemother by the hand. Suddenly, she stopped dead. "But how did you drive home without them? That's terribly dangerous, Alison."

The housemother's face took on an impish expression. "Not if you're wearing contacts, it isn't. I never have to push those glasses up my nose again. And a good thing, too — they were wearing a groove right between my eyes. All right, don't tell me — I'm the type who'll regress. Do you know I have to boil these lenses every night?"

Dana spoke for the first time. Her voice sounded hollow. "Why did you get contacts?" she asked slowly.

"Oh, just a change, I guess. Every other blind bat I know swears by them."

"Alison," Shelley said, "I love your new look." She glanced at Dana's sullen face and then at Faith's. They all knew — or thought they knew — the reason for Alison's transformation. And the reason had dark brown hair and laugh lines under his perceptive eyes.

"Well, I'm off. See you girls later," Alison smiled. As the housemother started up the stairs, Dana moved aside, turning her back abruptly. Alison was about to say something to her, but then, thought better of it. This wasn't the time or the place. The smile was gone from her face as she walked inside Baker.

"Want to go get ready for supper?" Faith asked, a little too cheerily. "I could eat a bear."

"Yeah, well you're in luck, because that's what they're serving tonight," Shelley laughed, trying as hard as she ever had to be funny. Dana didn't laugh, didn't crack a smile. Her grim face was set and determined as she walked into the dorm. There was something she had to do — and quickly.

The next morning, Dana was dressed and ready for chapel before anyone else. Her excuse was that she had to get there early to rehearse one of the hymns, but the truth of the matter was that she wanted some time alone. Dana had worked hard to get into the Canby Hall choir and had been thrilled beyond belief when she was accepted. She was a self-taught singer, and, unlike some of the other girls in the choir, had no experience at all with choral singing. But over the past year, as she grew accustomed to blending her strong, sweet alto with the other voices, she'd learned what teamwork was all about. Even now, as distracted as she was, she loved the Monday practice and Sunday performance. Just sitting in the choir loft high above the chapel, with its white walls, its stained-glass rainbow-colored windows and

its simple altar, made her feel good about life
in general. Things would work out, she
decided. They *had* to work out.

This morning, she sang her heart out,
letting the quiet hymns calm her troubled
soul. She looked down furtively to see if
Michael by any chance had wandered in to
sample a service, but he was nowhere in
sight. She knew he was Jewish, because he'd
mentioned it once, but lots of the Jewish
girls attended the ecumenical Canby Hall
service. Anyway, whatever his reason, he
hadn't come this morning.

At the end of the service, Dana grabbed
her music and starting down the circular
staircase that led from the choir loft to the
side door.

Even before her roommates could wander
across the campus back to Baker for the
Sunday brunch, Dana had changed into her
running gear. She left Faith and Shelley a
note on the door telling them not to wait for
her, and then she was off, sprinting toward
the East Faculty houses. As she rounded the
bend of the maple groves, she saw the red
bike. Michael was standing beside it.

"Hi!" she grinned, taking him all in at
a glance. He was dressed in a faded work-
shirt, which was open at the collar to reveal
a maroon turtleneck. His jeans were old and
comfortable-looking.

"How're you doing?" he asked, clearly
puzzled to see her. Since he'd fixed up his

office in the library, none of the students had been to his house. And although it was his style to develop easy, casual relationships with every girl he dealt with, he felt it was important that they not take advantage of him. Sunday was his day of rest.

"I'm okay. Can I come in? Or were you going out?"

"Just wandered to the back to look at my garden. Or what will be my garden when I turn the earth over." He paused and waited for her to speak, but she just stood there, looking anxious. "What can I do for you?" He opened the door and, after a minute, he showed her into the kitchen.

"I'm not disturbing you, am I?" Dana began speaking very quickly. "I thought maybe I'd see you at the chapel, but then I didn't so I figured if I wanted to get hold of you I'd better come over."

"Sounds logical." He scratched his chin, then straddled one of the kitchen chairs backwards. "Can I make you some tea?"

She shook her head. "But I might take a Coke, if you're having one."

He laughed sheepishly. "I'm afraid my larder is now permanently bare of Coke. I'm going cold turkey. Want some dried apricots?" He pushed the open baggie on the table toward her. She looked at it with loathing.

"What happened to your corn chips?"

"They have gone the way of all garbage," he sighed. "And more's the pity."

Dana's eyes narrowed. Was it possible that someone had persuaded Michael to go on a health kick? No, he was too much his own man for that. He'd probably just decided that it might be good for him. On the other hand, there was one person who would insist that Michael Frank give up junk food. Dana had prayed that the thing about Alison was just a rumor, and even yesterday, after the hair and the contacts, she still hoped. But her shred of hope was wearing very thin indeed.

"I only wanted to know if you're coming to the midwinter dance. I figured, since you're new here, you might not know it's traditional for faculty to come. So I thought it would be nice to invite you before you got busy doing something else. It's next Saturday night."

She had never invited anyone out before. Of course, it wasn't as if she was asking him on a date — she was already going with Randy — but just the audacity of inviting him startled her. She did things for Michael she wouldn't dream of doing for anyone else.

"Well, thanks. As it happens, I am coming," he smiled. "But I'm delighted to be asked again."

"Oh. I see. Who asked you?" she demanded bluntly, knowing but insisting that he punish her with the name.

"It was your housemother, actually. Alison Cavanaugh. And I got an all-points bulletin from Patrice Allardyce herself announcing that if I didn't show my face, I was in deep trouble."

"Well, good." Dana got up clumsily, nearly knocking her chair over. "I'll see you there."

"Will you save me a dance?" he asked softly.

At first, she thought she hadn't heard right, that she'd imagined it just because those were the very words she wanted him to say. But when she looked up into his wise eyes, she knew she wasn't dreaming. "Yes, of course," she breathed.

The rest of the week didn't happen at all. There was nothing for Dana but the Saturday to come.

CHAPTER SEVEN

"Well, hold still, will you, or I'll pin your shins instead of the fabric!" Faith was completely exasperated with her roommate.

"I can't help it," Shelley wailed. "Tom and Johnny will be here in ten minutes, and I'm not ready."

"But you look super — really you do," Dana smiled gently. She had lent Shelley her antique white angora sweater with tiny rhinestones on the collar, and Faith had supplied her with a tight, well-cut pair of black cords. The only problem was that Shelley stood about five inches shorter than Faith, and the pants legs lay like puddles around her feet. No matter the height of the heels she tried to totter around in, the pants refused to cooperate and look normal. Faith's solution was safety pins, but they weren't working at all.

"I've got it," Dana said, sitting up on her

bed and yanking at her own cowboy boots. "You'll tuck the pants into the boots. Now that's fashion." Dana had a way with clothes — her own flair for dressing was the envy of the dorm — and she often saved the day for Shelley by coming up with just the right outfit for a particular occasion. This was one of them.

"But *you* were going to wear the boots," Faith commented.

"It's okay, I've got some low ones that'll work," Dana said. She was floating on a cloud, scarcely aware of anything but her anticipation of the evening to come.

"Boy, you're a pal," Shelley sighed, putting on a second pair of socks. The boots were way too big for her, but tonight, that was unimportant. Even the blisters she knew she'd have the next morning didn't daunt her.

"It's incredible that you can fit into those cords," Faith stated as she gave Shelley a final once-over. "When you first came to school, your right leg couldn't have worn those pants," she chuckled.

"How true. I really was gross," Shelley frowned, whirling around to examine herself in the full-length mirror. She had just weighed herself that morning, and was delighted to find that she'd lost four pounds that week — one more than she'd intended. Going without her last two dinners and a lunch had been worth it.

The house phone buzzed out in the hallway, and they heard the running steps of Heather, the floor monitor, as she flew to her post.

"Which one is it?" Faith asked. "Any bets?"

"Johnny," Dana stated. "He's always early."

"Could be Randy. That pickup truck of his goes like the wind," Faith teased. The truth was that neither Shelley nor Faith had much hope for Dana's relationship with Randy Crowell. He was a Greenleaf farm boy, a local landowner's son who wasn't going on to college, and although that didn't rule him out, they both knew that Dana had interests Randy couldn't share with her. He was loyal, though, and very fond of Dana, and for that reason, the girls never got on her case about him.

"Shelley!" Heather called. "A gentleman caller!"

"Oh, my gosh! Tom! Have a good time, guys! See you at the ball!" With that, she was off and running, nearly tripping on the boots that had been her fashion salvation. She looked flushed and happy, although a little dizzy with excitement.

"Well, that's one down," Faith said as the buzzer rang again. "We might as well go on and wait for them in the lounge. Let's not stand on ceremony."

"Okay," Dana agreed. She hadn't given

much thought to how she was going to handle Randy, if handle was the right word. In the back of her mind, she was vaguely hoping that he'd want to dance with a lot of other people tonight — circulate more than he usually did at Canby Hall functions. Since graduating from Greenleaf High last year, Randy had been working for his father, tending horses and mending fences. Consequently, he didn't feel that he had much in common with "the schoolies," as he called them. But if he met a really great girl tonight, then Dana would be off the hook. She would still be his friend, of course, but it was pointless to think there could be anything else between them. Since she'd grown close to Michael, she'd placed Randy on an emotional back burner.

Dana and Faith walked down the stairs and were pleased to see Johnny and Randy coming in the front door together, shaking large, fat snowflakes off their collars.

"Well, look who's here," Johnny smiled, opening his arms to Faith. She went to him slowly, almost shyly. She wasn't used to being hugged in public, but with Johnny it was different. When his arms came around her, she snuggled close, lifting her face to his. Then, in front of Dana and Randy, he kissed her softly. Their lips clung together for the briefest moment — but it was very special to both of them. Faith thought Johnny Bates was a fantastic person, and she liked being

with him more than with any other boy she'd
ever known. But he wanted to be a cop — a
detective, actually. The fact of what had happened to her father, who had loved the law
and died for it, loomed over their relationship,
and every once in a while, Faith was tempted
to step back. She didn't want to love someone
who might put himself in terrible danger, not
ever again. And yet, she did love Johnny.
What could she do about that? He was a lean
whip of a boy, way over six feet tall, with
pecan-tan skin and a wide, generous smile.
His deep brown eyes were laughing tonight.
"You ready to dance your feet off, lady? Hey,
Dana — how're you doing?"

"Just fine, Johnny," Dana said. "Hi,
Randy." She walked over to him, and he
tilted back his wide-brimmed cowboy hat in
greeting. Randy didn't say much, but he certainly communicated. His face, tonight, was
puzzled, a little annoyed at her casual hello.
He'd expected something more.

"Well, shall we get going? Hope you girls
don't mind a little snow," Randy commented
as he helped Dana on with her parka and
opened the door, letting in a freezing blast
of air. The night sky was thick with whirling
flakes, and there was no sign that the storm
had any intention of letting up. The front
steps of Baker were already piled with white,
despite all the traffic of girls and their dates
on their way to the gym.

They hurried along the path without a

word, and Dana's breath quickened as she realized she was getting closer to *him*. She imagined what he'd wear, how his aftershave would smell when they swayed to the music, what he'd say. *"Why, Dana, I never knew you danced so beautifully, like a swan gliding on water. I asked you for one dance, but we can't stop now. Do you mind if we continue?"*

"Oh, Michael, of course I don't."

Then a little voice inside her spoke up. *Dana, you better watch it. This is all complete and utter idiocy, just your weird fantasy of how you'd like it to be. Anyhow, you've already got a date,* said the not-so-gentle reminder.

Other couples hurried by them, many girls complaining as they ran that their shoes and hair were going to be hopeless for the entire evening. Dana, on the other hand, was feeling silly and happy, for no apparent reason. As Randy took her by the hand and they broke into a run behind Johnny and Faith, she was simply elated — there was no other word for it. The snowflakes mingling with her long, dark lashes felt like stars in her shining eyes.

This was the first year that the Canby seniors had decided to go all out for the occasion, and it showed. As Dana entered the huge sports complex on Randy's arm, she gasped in admiration at the committee's work. The main gym had been transformed into a disco, with a live band made up of kids from town. They were already tuning up on the raised dais that had been decorated with sheets of silver Mylar. The rest of the room had been done in blue and white, the Canby school colors, but this was not your usual streamers-and-balloons job. The effect had been done with colored lights, one of which was a flashing blue strobe that hung down in the center like a chandelier. The Greenleaf florist, Mr. Atkins, had rented the decorating committee a dozen giant ferns, which gave the usually smelly, ugly gym an exotic, tropical cast.

"It's amazing what you can do with a little ingenuity, isn't it?" Faith marveled. "This place is a work of genius," she yelled to Johnny over the noise of the amplifiers.

"Who cares about geniuses tonight?" Johnny did a few fancy steps in place. "Take off that coat and let's boogie down!" With a backward glance at Dana, Faith allowed herself to be swept into the crowd. It was clear that she was ready for an evening of nonstop dancing.

"Sure is loud," Randy commented. "But I can take it if you can. How about it, Dana?" He made a courtly bow and missed the fact that she wasn't glancing at him, but was scanning the floor. Where was he? Had he come in yet?

But with all the ferns and bright lights, she could hardly see a thing. Everyone was painted with splotches of color when they weren't shadowed by the arch of a plant leaf. She would find him later, she told herself consolingly as she took Randy's hand and together, they penetrated the groups of dancers. The room, for all its size, was packed with people.

All the Canby girls were there, of course, except for Pamela and one or two others who'd been docked because of bad grades. Just that morning, Shelley had seen Pamela skulking around Baker's halls, "with a look on her face," she told Dana, "that would have curdled cream. I'm going to stay out of her way for a while," she'd decided.

As the band segued into a slow number, Dana felt Randy's arms steal around her and draw her close. She moved with him, but not in the comfortable way she usually did.

"Want to talk about it?" he asked quietly as they swayed together. Randy never suggested talking about anything, so Dana looked at him with great curiosity.

"About what?"

"Why you've been so standoffish lately. Why you don't want to see me. You thinking of moving onto another pasture?" He seemed mildly angry at her.

"Randy, for heaven's sake, why do you force everything into horse imagery?" She laughed, but it came out more like a croak.

"Cause horses are what I know. Also,

they're honest. Don't mess around with horses, lest you get kicked."

"Well, I'm not a horse, and I'm not in a kicking mood."

"I was talking about me," he said, stopping right in the middle of the dance. They both stood there as other couples jockeyed for position around them.

"I'm thirsty. Can we go get a Coke?" Dana said to break the silence. This was awful! She should never have let Randy invite himself. It was true — she *was* different with him now. There was simply no way not to let it show.

He shrugged and began edging his way over to the buffet table that had been set up along one wall of the gym. There were four seniors wearing blue-and-white aprons, pouring soda into plastic glasses and arranging chips and cookies on paper plates. Randy reached through several lines of students and plucked out two Cokes, managing to keep most of the liquid in the glasses.

"Oh, there's Shelley and Tom!" Dana said with relief, pointing to the far end of the table. "Let's go say hi." She didn't wait for Randy, but plowed ahead by herself. She knew she was acting terrible — she couldn't stand it when a boy treated her the way she was treating him — but she didn't seem to have any alternative. Shelley's face was an oasis in this desert of clamor and hurt feelings.

"Having fun?" Dana asked her roommate as Randy brought up the rear.

"This is really something," Tom stated emphatically, his booming voice just making it over the volume of the band. He put an arm around Shelley's shoulder and cupped his hand protectively over her ear. Tom and Shelley had met last spring when they were both cast in a Canby play, and the two of them were equally committed to a career in the theater. There was more to Tom than his typical young-leading-man aura, however. He was good for Shelley, and had been at least partly responsible for opening a new world to her. Before meeting Tom, her highest ambition had been to go home and marry the boy next door (Paul didn't really live next door, but close), and raise two point five kids. Now, she saw over the horizon — and she liked what she saw.

"It's probably the best dance I've ever attended," Shelley agreed, hopping from one foot to the next in time to the music. "Despite the size of these boots," she whispered to Dana. As she leaned over to get closer to her roommate, she missed her footing and nearly toppled over.

"Whoa!" Randy grabbed her arm, preventing her fall. "Take it easy."

"It must be the flashing lights — makes me dizzy. Doesn't it make you dizzy, Dana?" Shelley asked, embarrassed.

But Dana didn't answer. Across the floor,

gyrating in a circle pattern, was Michael Frank. His dark hair looked blue in the lights, and she could see the grin on his face as he twirled his partner under his arm. The woman being twirled was Alison Cavanaugh, and she looked very happy about it.

As Michael turned, he spotted Dana and her group and waved over Alison's head. Then he took his partner's hand and spun her in a circle. Her neatly cut hair swung back and forth under the arm of his tweed jacket. The sight made Dana's stomach cramp.

The band slowed down only to speed up in its next number to a more furious pace. Dana saw Alison shaking her head and pushing Michael toward someone else. She squinted, peering through a fern to see who his new partner was. She was short and blonde and . . . Casey! It was Casey, who'd proclaimed earlier that day that she intended to dance with every single man in the room.

"You interested in making some moves with me?" Tom asked Dana. Before she could answer, Shelley took Randy's hand and led him onto the floor. Dana had no choice then but to nod at Tom and let him spin her back into the crowd.

Tom danced well, much better than Randy, in fact, but Dana wasn't concentrating on her partner's fluid movements. She saw only Michael. There he was, grinding his feet into the floor beside Mary Beth Grover, whose

usually pale face was now flushed and eager.
When she bowed out, he asked Ellie Bolton
to dance, and after her came Heather and
Tracy, the art director of the Canby *Clarion*.
He danced with both girls at the same time,
and the three of them kept tripping over each
other because they were laughing so hard.

The number ended, and Tom was about to
lead her off the floor when Dana felt a tap
on her shoulder.

"May I?" asked Michael.

"You may," she smiled, and her smile lit
up the room. The band began to play, "You
Are The Sunshine Of My Life," and she
melted into his arms, not too close but near
enough to feel the rough wool cloth of his
jacket against her cheek. She pronounced a
silent blessing on the band for playing a
slow song.

They didn't speak; they didn't have to.
Dana felt her senses meld together as they
danced as one person, just the way they ran
together. She was aware of so many things
— his hand holding her back so lightly, the
other fitting like a glove over her own. His
muscular body, trim and fit from all those
miles he'd covered over the years, swaying
gently against her, making her feel faint and
giddy. The scent of him, clean and new, as
though he'd just stepped out of a shower.
And most of all, the way he looked when she
gazed into his eyes. The two of them were
so nearly the same height that she didn't

have to look up to see the expression on his face.

Was this the first time they'd ever touched? she wondered as her hand began to tingle. No, that first day, when she came to his house, he'd given her a friendly handshake in greeting. But tonight, his hand was warmer, fonder, as though it almost knew how important this moment was to her. And would be to her, forever. When she was old and gray, when she had accomplished what she intended in life, when she had retired from her successful career and had children and grandchildren of her own, this evening would still be one of her most memorable experiences. Tears of joy stung her eyes as she realized how lucky she was, how wonderful it was to be Dana Morrison.

"You look like you're enjoying yourself tonight," he commented. "That fellow you came with seems like quite a catch."

"Randy's just a friend," she explained hastily. "He's really too young for me," she added.

Michael pulled back a bit, peering into her face to see if she was joking. When he saw that she wasn't, he nodded solemnly and said, "I see."

"You think that's dumb, don't you? To worry about whether he's more mature than me — or vice versa?"

"I didn't say that." His smile was teasing, though. She knew he was attempting to make her laugh at herself.

"You didn't have to."

"Dana, when I got into college, I was a year younger than everybody else. Mind you, it was due to no brilliance on my part; I'd just started grade school early because my birthday fell on the cut-off date and my mother was itching to get me out of the house."

She laughed, trying to imagine his mother.

"Anyhow, I got to college, and there were all these girls. It was mind-boggling. I tried everything under the sun and a few things I made up all by myself, but try as I might, I couldn't get a date. And I bet every one of those girls said I was too young for them."

"How *could* they!" She was immediately indignant, furious with those long-ago heart-breakers who'd scorned him.

"What they actually said was that I was too short. I was a shrimp till the end of my sophomore year." He sighed and turned them both in a circle.

The band started to play the reprise of the number, and Dana's mood plummeted. It was ending! She couldn't let him go — not now.

"You know how to dip?" Michael's smile crept down her body, in between her toes like warm sand on a hot summer's day. "Ready? Okay, here we go!" He bent her over gracefully, letting her fall back in his arms. She was lightheaded, about to swoon.

This was how it was supposed to feel, this lovely, unsettling merry-go-round of emotions and expectations. This was the real thing.

"Oh, no! Somebody help! Get over here fast!"

Dana jerked upright and snapped to attention as the crowd in the middle of the floor parted at the sound of the boy's shout. What was going on? The band's last notes trailed off unevenly. Michael grabbed her hand and nearly dragged her across the dance floor to the spot where at least ten couples were grouped around a figure who was lying, sprawled in a heap.

"Move aside! Make way!" He pushed some of the taller boys aside and, as they got to the edge of the circle, Dana saw who it was. She gasped and rushed forward. Shelley was lying there unconscious, her face frozen in a white mask of fear. Tom was kneeling beside her.

"What is it? What happened?" Faith was trying to get through, and the crowd parted for her.

"She passed out," Tom murmured. "Just went limp and fell over."

"Let's get her to the infirmary." Alison's strong voice cut through the hubbub. "Tom, help Michael get her up. All right everyone, it's all over now. Go back to your dancing. Go ahead."

Slowly, the couples reassembled and the

band struck up the next number. Dana and
Faith raced ahead to open the gym doors for
Michael and Tom, who had made a chair
of their hands for Shelley. Johnny and
Randy followed them out into the night,
which was a perfect blend of black sky and
swirling white snow.

"I've got a blanket in the truck," Randy
called as he ran ahead. "Let's cover her up."

The others, standing in the doorway,
huddled protectively over their charge while
Randy ran ahead for the blanket. Alison's
face was firm and set as she looked from
Dana to Faith and back again. "What hit
her? Do you know?"

Nobody had a clue. They all looked anxiously at Shelley, who was leaning against
the doorframe, pale as death. She was still
out cold.

CHAPTER EIGHT

"Zennie, keep her in that bed and keep her warm," Michael instructed Ms. Zenger, the school nurse.

"I know what to do," Zennie said between pursed lips. She was so neat and orderly, even her gray hair looked starched under its pristine white cap. "All of you move aside." She shoved Dana, Faith, and the three boys down the corridor as though they were pesky insects.

"Please," Dana protested. "We have to be with her."

"We're her best friends," Faith added. "We should stay until she wakes up."

"And I have to be with her," Tom insisted. "I'm her boyfriend."

Alison put an arm around each of the girls, pointing them and Tom toward the door. "Why don't we give her a few minutes to just lie there. You guys can sit in the waiting area, and as soon as she comes around, Zennie will call you." She glanced meaningfully at the nurse.

"I'd like to look in on her," Michael said quietly. His handsome face looked older in the harsh overhead lights. "I'll be right out." He walked into the small white room, closed the door behind him, and pulled a chair to the side of the bed. At the sound of his step, Shelley's eyes fluttered open.

"Well, good morning," Michael said.

"Oh, no! Oh, this is terrible. I just made a complete fool of myself, right?" She buried her face in her hands. "Right in the middle of the dance. Oh, how utterly horrible!" The color came back into her face as she realized what must have happened. "I could feel myself falling, and I couldn't stop it." She peered through her fingers at him. "I'm so embarrassed." As she started to raise up on one elbow, Michael pushed her back down.

"Stay right there," he instructed her.

"But I'm okay now," she assured him. "Really."

"Shelley," he said softly, "when was the last time you ate?"

"What!" She bit her lip and looked at the wall.

"It seems to me, although I don't want to jump to any conclusions, that you might have passed out because you were weak from not eating. Answer me truthfully." He was stern with her, not scolding, but determined to get to the bottom of this. He was also very concerned.

"I skipped lunch and dinner today," she admitted. "And dinner last night. That's all."

He crossed his arms and looked at her, encouraging her to go on.

"I just wanted to lose a couple of pounds so I could fit into Faith's pants. That's all it was. I lost a few more than I intended," she stammered. Then, suddenly, she burst out crying. "I'm sorry — please don't be angry with me. I didn't mean it."

"Shelley," he said gently, "when we talked, you told me you liked the way you looked. And when your mom sent up those cookies, I saw you eat two of them, right in front of me."

"Three," she sniffed, rubbing her nose. "But I gave the rest away as soon as I got back to the dorm."

"Are you upset about something? Problems with grades? With your boyfriend?"

"No!" She frowned and shook her head. "I mean, sometimes I feel like I'm under a lot of pressure. Like when I audition for plays or compete on the swim team. Maybe it's just being with so many kids who are really talented and sophisticated, you know? They're so. . . ." She searched for a word. "Some of them are so *perfect*."

"Just the way you'd like to be?" he asked.

"I guess," she admitted.

"Well, getting skinny won't make you any more perfect," he told her quietly. "The only thing that does is make you very sick."

"I know," she whispered. "I'm sorry."

"All right." He moved his chair so he could sit in his favorite position, which was balanced back on two legs. "How about this? You come and have dinner at my house every night for the next week, or however long we decide. You can bring Faith and Dana if you like. But it's an appointment for you, not just an invitation. We're going to try to get you to think differently about food, and what it means to you, okay? Maybe that'll be easier if we do it together." He grinned, and his tone lightened considerably. "I've got the expert health nut teaching me to cook, by the way, and she'll see to it that we all stick to our guns."

"Alison, you mean?" Shelley asked.

"Right. So, how does this sound to you?"

She thought about it for less than a second. "It sounds good. I really don't want to do this to myself."

"I know you don't." He reached out and covered the cold, little hand that lay on top of the blanket. "Get some sleep. I'll have Zennie bring you some broth a little later."

"Sure," she smiled.

He got up and went to the door, pausing once to look at her again. "You don't have to tell Faith and Dana what's going on unless you want to. But it could be helpful to have a cheering section."

"Thanks, Michael. I'll tell them tomorrow — we do share everything, after all." She smiled at him gratefully. "You know, you're really wonderful."

"Ain't I just?" he grinned.

When he was gone, she turned over and hugged the pillow to her chest as she made a solemn vow to herself. She would stop being so self-critical, stop feeling so pressured about every little thing. And she would go back to eating normally.

Dana stopped in first thing in the morning to check on her, and Shelley told all, much to her roommate's shock and disbelief. "Shel, that's terrible. I just thought you were dieting. From now on, we'll have to take better care of you."

"No," Shelley said in a firm voice, "I have to take better care of myself. But I need you to root for me."

Faith came later that morning with Casey. Alison was bustling around the infirmary room, opening the window shades to let in some light. The snow had finally let up a little, but there was at least a foot on the ground.

"Boy," Casey said as she plopped down at the foot of Shelley's bed. "You really are a kook." Faith came over and hit her on the head. "Ow! I mean, you're not," Casey laughed. "You're more normal than all of us put together. But sometimes you act like a dodo."

Faith pushed Casey aside and started clucking over Shelley like a mother hen. "I wish you'd said something sooner. I wish I'd seen that there was something wrong."

Shelley shook her head and looked at the three of them. "You're all grand to care so much, but honest, you couldn't have done a thing. I've been talking to Michael about it, and I think I've got it under control. So." She pulled her knees up to her chest and grinned conspiratorially. "What'd I miss? How was the rest of the dance?"

It was evident from the looks on everyone's faces that the topic of Shelley hadn't been exhausted, but they respected her wish that they stop harping on it. Casey was the best of them all at switching from tragedy to comedy in a split second.

"That dance was totally marvelous," she sighed. "I met at least four men I could spend the rest of my life with."

Alison snickered and came over to sit on the other side of the bed. "You sure are fortunate, Case. Here I am at 26, still struggling to find *one*."

Faith and Shelley exchanged looks. "But Alison," Casey teased, "it looks to us like something may be in the cards for you, might be right on your very doorstep."

She couldn't have put it any more succinctly. Alison's face turned the same shade as her lipstick. "Well. . . ."

"Well?" Shelley prompted.

"I know what you're all thinking," she confessed. "And according to you, I'm sure, Michael Frank is a perfect man, right?"

Three heads nodded vehemently.

"There's no such thing," Alison said quickly. "It has taken me this many years to discover that."

There was a knock at the door, and Tom appeared as it opened slowly. He looked awfully worried. "May I come in?"

"Sure," Alison smiled. "Speaking of men . . ." she added as she ushered Faith and Casey out the door.

"See you later, Shel," the two girls chorused. Then they walked slowly down the hall, pulling on their coats and hats as they went.

"I think this thing with Michael is more serious than Alison says," Casey decided as they stepped into the cold winter's day.

"I agree," Faith nodded. "Poor Dana."

Dana's mind was in what she liked to call "mix-master condition" all that day. She was still floating on a cloud of dreamy remembrances, twirling endlessly on a dance floor with Michael. But she was terribly upset about Shelley, and about her own lack of perception. She'd thought she knew her roommates so well, that she could read their every wish and trouble. And yet here she'd missed something so urgent. It made her feel selfish and petty. How could she have let her own problems take precedence over everything, even friendship?

And something else was eating at her. What was really going on with Alison? She could rationalize that her housemother and the guidance counselor were just good friends, because after all, they were about the same age and had certain things in common; she could tell herself that Michael was really more interested in the young, sparkling girl who'd become his running partner, but was she fooling herself? If only she could ask him.

The final problem was Randy. She couldn't let this hang anymore — it was just so unfair. About midday, she dug down deep in her pocket and pulled out a dime. Reluctantly, as though she were walking to an execution, she marched downstairs to the phones and made the call.

"Hi, how are you this morning?" she asked cheerily when he answered.

"Not too bad. How's that roommate of yours?" His voice was calm, unruffled as usual.

"I guess she's all right."

"Good thing."

There was a silence that seemed endless. You could have fit Beethoven's Fifth Symphony into that space if you tried hard.

"Well, I was just wondering if you might be up for a pizza this afternoon," Dana blurted out. "Maybe we could meet and talk."

"Okay by me."

Why was he so unaffected? It was one of the things about him that drove her buggy! The guy just didn't know how to use the English language!

"How's four o'clock?" she asked, annoyed that he was forcing her to do all the work.

"Okay by me. See you."

She hung up in a snit, more certain than ever that she had to end this relationship. Not only was he immature, he just didn't understand her at all. She'd made that phone call because she felt rotten about the way she'd been behaving to Randy lately, but at this moment, she didn't feel the least bit of remorse. Nothing seemed to get to him anyway, so why should she worry about him? She'd get to Pizza Pete's, order a Coke, and just tell him she didn't want to see him anymore. Period.

As she was walking back up toward the lounge, she walked smack into Pamela Young, who was on her way out the door. She had on her mink-collared cape today, and a sweet little beige cashmere beret. Pamela faced her with a truly delighted smile.

"Why, Dana, the *very* person I was looking for!"

"Oh?" This had to be something bad — she could feel it coming.

"I was just *so* worried about Shelley. I heard what happened last night — unfortunately, I had a prior engagement, so I couldn't make it to the dance — but that was just *awful!*"

Prior engagement, my foot! She was docked! Dana thought. Aloud, she said. "It's awfully nice of you to ask, Pamela, but there's nothing the matter, actually. She's fine now."

"Oh, don't believe it," Pamela said in a hushed, sepulchral tone. "Once they start not eating, you can't *stop* them." She put one party-pink nail on Dana's arm. "You better watch her."

Dana didn't even answer her — there was no point. But as she started to pass her on her way up the staircase, Pamela threw her another bombshell.

"Boy, everybody's got problems these days. I understand the guidance counselor's on his way out. Did you hear that?"

"What? What are you talking about?" Dana turned on her, her bright green eyes flashing.

"Well, it's not surprising, after all. You know, it's against the law in this state to betray a kid's confidence. But that Michael Frank just can't keep his mouth shut. Too bad, really. He sure is a hunk!" With a sly little smile on her face, she waltzed down the steps. Even when Dana stopped her, holding her shoulder with a grip that would have bent steel, Pamela's smile didn't fade.

"Betraying confidences! You're out of your mind!"

"Why, Dana, you should know better than anyone. Didn't you two discuss *me*?"

Dana felt something snap inside her. "But you . . . you asked me to do that! You begged me!" It was unbelievable to her that anyone could be this devious and cruel.

"Isn't it a *shame*? Sometimes when you mean to do something *really* good, it turns out being just the opposite." Pamela's eyes were cold, like a lizard's.

But Dana wasn't fazed. "I want to know what you're up to," she said between clenched teeth. "You tell me right this instant." She'd never been so furious in her life.

"You don't think I'd let some dumb faculty member ruin my whole life, do you?" Pamela said with fury. "I have connections, after all. He's not going to get away with having me expelled. I'll take him right along with me." And with that, she wrenched free of Dana, ran down the stairs, and out the door, her wide cape swirling behind her.

Dana couldn't catch her breath. Everything was churning inside her, but the primary emotion was terror. What was this awful girl capable of?

She gripped the banister, making her mind

function. What could she do to stop Pamela?
The first thing was to get to the person in
authority before it was too late. That meant
an audience with the headmistress, Patrice
Allardyce.

Dana shivered as she thought of the
haughty, austere woman who ran Canby
Hall with a strict adherence to everything
that was right and proper. The girls tried
hard to stay out of her way, and here was
Dana, bound right for her doorstep. She ran
back to her room, grabbed her parka, and
was out the door. The snow made no difference to her — she ran like the wind.

CHAPTER NINE

She'd gone as far as the wishing pond on the other side of the park that fronted Baker House when she heard someone calling her name.

"Oh, not *now*!" she muttered under her breath, but she stopped long enough to turn and look back. Faith was waving her arms wildly over her head as she tried to catch up with her long-legged roommate.

"Just a sec!" Faith sprinted the remaining distance and clutched at Dana as she collapsed in a mound of snow. "Whew! Lifting weights clearly doesn't prepare one for running marathons. You're not really jogging in all this cotton candy, are you? I wanted to talk about Shelley."

Dana pulled her friend to her feet, too tired herself to run any further. "That has to wait. Not that it's not important, but I'm in the midst of an emergency. Pamela Young is trying to get Michael fired."

"She's what!" Faith looked at the sky and lifted her hands in supplication. "Oh, will someone please buy that girl a one-way ticket to Eastern Siberia? I mean, I don't wish any evil to befall her; I just want her to take a nice long walk off a very short pier."

"Look, I've got to get to Allardyce and tell her the truth before Pamela does any serious damage. I can't stand here talking." Dana was already walking briskly in the direction of the headmistress's house.

"You better tell me what this is all about," Faith said, hurrying along beside her. "Anyhow, you can't confront Allardyce alone. You know she eats little girls for lunch." Actually, no one was ever sure how kind or how horrible the headmistress might be. The air of mystery in which she cloaked herself, however, gave everyone the impression that it was probably healthiest to stay out of her way.

"It's silly for you to come with me, though. This is my problem."

Faith took Dana's arm and whirled her around to face her. "Hey, I thought we three decided a long time ago that all our problems were communal property. That's how Shel got into so much trouble — by not confiding in us. Don't *you* start."

Dana bit her lip and thought for a second. "All right. Here it is. Pamela asked me to use my influence — well, that's what *she* called it, anyway — with Michael to go easy on her. It seems that he's the ultimate authority when it comes to expelling kids around here, because he can decide if they really want to improve their grades or if they've just got a chronic bad attitude — in which case, they should be out on their ear. Stupid me, I was flattered that she thought he'd listen to me, so I agreed. Turns out it was one of her nasty tricks. It's against the law for a guidance counselor to discuss one student with another. Not that we did any more than mention her name, of course. I wouldn't waste my breath discussing Pamela, but she told Allardyce that's what happened."

"They don't make humans lower than her, you know," Faith scowled.

"So I have to tell Allardyce that Pamela lied. I don't like doing it, but there you are." She turned and started walking again.

"Dana," Faith pointed out. "She didn't lie. I mean, all she'd have to say was that her name came up in your conversation."

"But that's absurd, it's —"

"We're talking facts here, girl. And while we're at it, do you really think you're the best candidate for defending Michael Frank? I think it would be better if I did it, or even Casey or Shel."

"What do you mean?"

"You're too personally involved, that's what I mean. Dana, I want you to listen to this without blowing up, because I'm going to say something that may not feel so good. But you're acting real goony over this guy. Ever heard of puppy love?"

Dana just stared at her. "I can't believe you. I'm trying to save a person's reputation, and you're accusing me of a silly infatuation."

"Well, what would you call it?" Faith demanded.

"I like him, yes. I respect him enormously. I think he's smart and perceptive and very good for all of us. I'm glad he came to Canby Hall and I want him to stay here."

They had reached the brick path that led to Patrice Allardyce's door, and both girls stopped, looking at the imposing doorway with a certain amount of dread.

"I don't think you have a clear-thinking bone in your body right now, but I'm with you. I believe the man's all right," Faith sighed, "so I'll go in there and beard the lioness with you." This was Faith's attempt at a joke, since the lioness was the school mascot, but neither of them even smiled.

Dana went to the door and rang the bell. Then they waited.

"She's not in. Let's go," Faith whispered.

But just at that moment, Patrice Allardyce herself flung open the door. She was a tall, elegant woman in her early forties, with a tight French twist of almost white-blonde hair smoothed off her high forehead. Unlike everyone else on campus, Ms. Allardyce did not dress down on Sundays. Today she was wearing a turquoise silk blouse with an ascot and trim black wool slacks.

"Yes, girls?" She was clearly puzzled to see them.

"We'd, ah . . . if you're not too busy, we'd like to speak with you," Dana stuttered. "If it's not convenient, we can come back. But it's enormously important," she added.

"You didn't make an appointment," Ms. Allardyce pointed out, "but I suppose this once, that can be forgiven. Come in. Please be brief and to the point," she reminded them as she led them into her living room. The last time Faith had been in there was when Casey had run away from school, and Dana had been there when she'd been spying on Ms. Allardyce. Being inside Ms. Allardyce's home was a privilege or a punishment, depending on the occasion. Everyone agreed, though, that her living room was nothing like her —filled with cozy armchairs and a flowered chintz-covered sofa, it might almost have belonged to a fun-loving, motherly type.

The girls were shown to two chairs in front of the fireplace, which was glowing with the warm embers of a dying fire. The headmistress put another log on, stirred things up a bit, and went over to sit across from them on the sofa. "Now," she prompted, "what's so important?"

"It's the guidance counselor, Michael

Frank," Dana said quickly. "There have been some rumors spread about him that simply aren't true."

Ms. Allardyce's impassive face did not change. "And how can you be so certain of that?"

"Because I *know* him. I know what he's capable of."

Faith gave her a despairing look. That was not the answer to the question. "She means that the particular incident that . . . *someone* may have mentioned to you has been blown all out of proportion, Ms. Allardyce. And Mr. Frank and Dana really should have the opportunity to tell you just what happened."

The headmistress looked away, as if none of this really interested her. "I take it you girls are here because you think you have some knowledge of the situation. But I'm afraid that I must handle student-faculty problems as I see fit. It's really no concern of yours. Thank you for coming by." She dismissed them, getting up to go to the door.

"No, please, Ms. Allardyce," Dana begged, her face distraught and white, "you have to listen to me before you do something you'll regret."

"You have no way of knowing what I intend to do, my dear," the older woman pointed out.

"But don't you have to hear all sides of a story?" Faith prompted. "In our society, isn't somebody innocent until proven guilty?"

That stopped her. She looked confused for a moment, and then she walked over to them, looking from one to the other. "Do you know what's been said to me in regard to this matter?" she asked.

"I think I do." Dana took a breath, and then continued. "Someone has accused Michael Frank of blabbing about one student to another. I mean, about not keeping his sessions confidential. And that's completely untrue."

"I see. Well, perhaps you're right. And then again, maybe you're not. Perhaps the best way to get to the truth of the matter is to interview all parties involved. That would be the best way. Why don't you both come back tomorrow at four? We'll have it out then."

"I wasn't really a part of this, Ms. Allardyce," Faith said. "I just came to be with Dana. But if Michael Frank needs a character witness, count me in," she added with a smile.

"That won't be necessary. All right then, just you, Dana. Tomorrow. The other two will be here," she added as the girls got up and she led them to the door.

"Thank you, Ms. Allardyce." Dana felt a huge load slide halfway off her shoulders. It wouldn't be completely gone until Michael was cleared, but at least this was a start.

"Thank you for coming," the headmistress

said, the perfect model of manners and propriety.

"Boy," Faith said when they were down the path and on their way back to Baker, "there could be a nuclear holocaust and that woman would still find time to say 'please' and 'thank you.' "

"Maybe that's not so bad, though," Dana said thoughtfully. "The world could stand a few more people who think before they talk. Maybe she's not so bad." She pulled her parka up around her ears as the wind whipped around them. "At least, I hope she's fair," she whispered. "For Michael's sake, and for mine."

The walk to Greenleaf had never seemed as long as it did that afternoon. The weather had swiftly deteriorated, and instead of a delightful fairytale snowfall, the girls had mean old Jack Frost biting at their noses, ears, and toes. It usually took twenty minutes to get from the Canby Hall gates to the town hall. Today, it took forty.

"I hope we're not late," Dana sighed to Casey as they trudged along, their heads down and shoulders hunched. "When you're going to tell a guy it's over, you shouldn't be late."

"Why not? Hey, I say, be as late as possible — let *him* be the one to call it quits. Dana, are you sure you're taking the right step here?" With that, she put her foot into a large hole that was covered with snow and fell right through.

"My step has to be better than yours," Dana laughed. It was, she realized, the first time she'd laughed since she'd been with Michael the previous night.

"But you like Randy. And he's a nice guy. Just because your eye has sort of lighted on something exotic and unusual doesn't mean you have to give up your daily routine, you know. Nobody says you have to have one or the other at your age. At our age," she corrected herself.

Dana frowned and looked over at her friend. "That's the second time today somebody's accused me of being head over heels. It's completely untrue." She was lying through her teeth.

"Dana, I didn't accuse you of anything. But Faith and Shelley and I can see that heart you're wearing on your sleeve, even if you can't. I just have to tell you that if you leave it there, it's gonna get a big hole punched right in the middle of it. Whereas with Randy —"

They'd just reached the outskirts of town when Randy's pickup truck zoomed around the bend. He saw the girls and pulled over at once. "C'mon, climb in. What are you doing walking around in this cold?"

"Coming to see you," Casey said calmly. She reached over and gave Dana's hand a squeeze. "You two go on," she said kindly.

"I'll continue on foot. Got to practice being an icicle for drama class," she said seriously to Randy. Then she shuddered, wrapped her arms around her slight frame, and moved on. Dana gave her a funny little smile and turned to climb up in the cab beside Randy.

"She's a nut, don't mind her," she explained.

"I know that already," he grinned. "You up for that pizza?"

"I guess," she nodded. She wished she didn't have so much on her mind at once. Of primary importance, of course, was the meeting with Michael tomorrow. She would have to try and find him early tomorrow so they could talk before they had to appear at Allardyce's with Pamela. Then there was Shelley. Dana didn't know how worried she was supposed to be about her roommate. And what about those comments Faith and Casey had made today about her feelings toward Michael? Should she pay any attention to them? It was hard to concentrate on what she'd wanted to tell Randy with so many other things to think about.

"Gone again," she heard Randy say as he parked the truck and reached across her to open the door.

"What? Oh, sorry. I am a little preoccupied."

"So I've noticed. Dana, if you can't give me your undivided attention for an hour, then it's plain dumb to go eat pizza," he said bluntly.

She was brought up short by her own rudeness. Randy might not be the boy of her dreams, and they might have very little in common, but he did deserve some common decency on her part. "I'm sorry," she said simply.

She let him lead her inside the bustling restaurant, which was crowded, as it was all weekend and some weeknights, with kids from Canby Hall, Oakley Prep, and Greenleaf High.

"What'll it be, kids?" Sally, the waitress, had the glasses of water and menus down on the table even before Randy and Dana were seated.

"A small mushroom pizza, Sally," Randy said.

"Can you make me some hot chocolate, Sally?" Dana asked.

"For you, kid, anything." The waitress left them in their booth, and Dana grabbed her glass of water for security. She drank half of it before she said another word.

"I guess you want to know why I wanted to talk," she murmured.

"I know. Say it anyway."

"I just don't think. . . . Oh, Randy, I like you so much, but I —" She stopped, realizing that anything she said would be hurtful. Earlier, when she got off the phone with him, she hadn't cared, but now, seeing him face to face, she knew this was a rotten thing to do.

"You like me, but you like someone else better. That it?" he prompted.

"No, really, it has nothing to do with anybody else. This is just between us. I feel that I'm. . . . Suddenly I need my privacy. I need to just think my own thoughts for a while, and not have them bump up against someone else's. Does that make sense?"

"None at all." His clear gray eyes were dull and lifeless. He had known this was coming, but he hadn't expected to take it so hard. "I'm not gonna fight you on this, Dana. Wouldn't do me a lick of good if I tried. But just because you got thoughts that I never have, doesn't mean we can't talk about them, or even argue about them. There's nothing wrong with two people being real different. You should hear my mom and dad sometimes."

For some reason, the mention of his family did it. Dana crumbled inside. What about her parents? She'd been so busy with her ninety-seven varieties of problems, she hadn't even thought about the weekend she was due to spend with her father and Eve. Or about what her mother and her sister Maggie were up to. She hadn't written a letter home in weeks, and had spoken to them only once on the phone.

"I'm sorry, Randy. I really am. But I need some time."

He shrugged, then slapped down some money on the table for the food that hadn't yet arrived. "You got it, lady. All the time you need. Good luck to you." Then he was gone, and Dana was sitting there all alone when Sally came back with the pizza.

"Don't tell me!" The waitress didn't even put the hot tin down on the table. "Suddenly, neither of you are hungry. No matter, don't worry, keep the change. Just so happens that other couple wanted a small mushroom pizza." She jerked her finger across the room, and Dana followed her glance to the two people sitting together in the front booth.

Her stomach felt as though someone had been using it for a punching bag. It wasn't enough that Randy had walked out on her, leaving all those hard words in his wake; it wasn't enough that Michael hadn't come in alone. The capper was that pizza. Michael was sitting there, about to share *her* pizza with Alison.

CHAPTER TEN

Dana didn't think anything could restore her good humor, probably ever. But she knew she was wrong, as soon as she got back to the dorm and saw Shelley sitting up in the window of Room 407, munching on one of Faith's imported-from-Washington, D.C. soft pretzels.

"When did you get back?" she asked breathlessly as she burst into the room, her cheeks rosy from the bite of the wind.

"About an hour ago. I told Zennie I was going stir-crazy, and Alison wasn't there to ask, so she just used her own judgment and released me. I'm really feeling much better, Dana."

Dana grinned and went over to her roommate, her arms spread for a hug. "Boy, did you give us a scare! But it's good to have you back. It's more than good — it's the only way." The two girls clung together for a moment, each realizing how much she needed the other.

Shelley was filled with so many emotions — with embarrassment, with love for her roommate, with gratitude that there were people around who cared enough not to let her get carried away with her own stupidity. "So," she said, pulling back a little, "how are *you*? I'm sick of talking about me."

Dana wrinkled up her nose and laughed sheepishly. "Oh, as well as can be expected, under the circumstances."

"What does that mean?" Shelley frowned.

"You may as well know," Dana sighed. "Everything's rotten. I feel totally lousy about ignoring you. I was all wound up in what was going on with me, but that's no excuse."

"Is that all?" Shelley scoffed. "I wasn't thinking about you or Faith or anything except fitting into a dumb pair of pants. I guess we were both pretty selfish. All right, what else?"

"It turns out, while we were being selfish, Pamela has become public enemy number one — for a change. And to top it all off, I think I just blew it with Randy."

"Gee," Shelley grimaced. "I go away for a few hours and the world falls apart. Okay, let's start from problem one and move on. I'm all ears."

For the next hour, the girls talked strategy. Shelley was dumbfounded and horrified to hear about Pamela's accusations, and she was ready to go storming over to Ms. Allardyce's house that very evening and defend Michael to the hilt. Then Faith walked in and they started from scratch on a calmer note. Faith had the ability to make her two headstrong roommates stop and think before going crazy. They discussed the upcoming meeting that Dana had to go to the following afternoon, and decided that her best course of action, and the one that would be most helpful to Michael, would be telling the facts, ma'am, just the facts. No tears, no heroics.

The girls wanted to hear all about what had happened with Randy, but Dana got cold feet when his name came up again. She was terribly confused about what she'd done, and she certainly didn't feel good about it. She promised to share it with Faith and Shelley after she'd sorted it out for herself.

About an hour later, Faith happened to glance at the clock. "Oh, m'gosh, the dining room's about to close."

"How I wish it would close permanently," Dana snickered. "Then we wouldn't have to eat that stuff. I'm sure it causes brain damage."

Shelley led the way to the dining hall and proceeded to consume a huge portion of lasagna and a large salad, chased down by a large glass of milk and a piece of apple pie. The crisis, it seemed, was over.

"Listen, Michael's cooking for me the rest of this week," she smiled, "and he's invited both of you to come, too. Apparently he wants to make sure I'm on the right track before letting me loose. He's into health food now, you know."

"Well, if he'd seen you tonight, he'd cancel the invitation. I don't think you need much encouragement. What's he cooking?" Faith asked suspiciously. "Wheat germ and seaweed?"

Dana wondered whether mushroom pizza could be vaguely construed as healthy. She didn't think so.

"I don't know, but I don't have a choice. So come with me." She glanced from Faith to Dana, and they both nodded at once. Dana didn't want to go and eat at Michael's house, but for Shelley, she'd risk it. Even if Alison were there.

"Oh, yuk. Look who just walked in," Faith muttered. The others glanced over to the door of the dining hall, where Faith's eyes were riveted.

"It's that traitor, Pamela," Faith breathed. "I really don't want to sit in the same room with her. Let's get out of here before I feel impelled to use some of my new muscles." In a huff, she pushed back from the table. As Dana followed her over to the tray return, she didn't look back. She knew what she had to do tomorrow, and she was determined to succeed.

* * *

There was simply too much to do on Monday morning, so it was lunchtime before Dana could get to Michael's office.

There was a note on his door announcing that he'd gone out and would be back later in the afternoon — no mention was made of the exact hour.

"Oh, no!" Dana muttered. It would be four before she knew it, and she'd have to go into that meeting cold, without even a word to him. For all she knew, he might think *she* was behind this terrible business. No, that was absurd, he wouldn't think that, but she didn't know *what* he thought, and that bothered her. She was worried about him.

At the appointed hour, she smoothed her long, dark hair, crossed her fingers for luck, and started over to Ms. Allardyce's house. She prayed she wouldn't run into Pamela on the way, but of course, it was difficult to arrive neither too early nor too late and still avoid the object of her hatred.

Pamela was ringing the bell when she came up the walk.

"Well, hello." She smiled smugly at Dana, who didn't say a thing. "Guess we have a big decision to make, don't we?"

"Yes," Dana responded. "Whether to lie, or tell the truth."

The door opened in Pamela's surprised face, and Ms. Allardyce showed them both into the living room. Michael was sitting in one of the easy chairs by the fire, and he rose as the three of them entered the room.

"Have a seat, girls," Ms. Allardyce said. Pamela went directly to the sofa, and Dana moved as far from her as she could get, all the way to the chair on the opposite end of the room. Unfortunately, this also placed her very far from Michael.

"I don't have to preface my remarks with a warning that this is very serious business," the headmistress said, looking at both girls with steely eyes. She had a way of communicating more with a glance than she did with a whole paragraph. "I think you're aware of that. I've discussed the matter with Mr. Frank, but he is interested in hearing all sides, just as I am. Pamela, since you are the one making the accusation, I suggest that you begin."

"Of course, Ms. Allardyce." She cleared her throat, the very image of a self-assured, confident young woman. "As you know, I was asked to see the guidance counselor about my grades. It was nothing, really," she said, quickly covering for herself, "but I was certainly glad that we got things straightened out. But then, I learned from Dana that when she had her session with Michael — with Mr. Frank — he'd told her all about my academic standing. Now, really, do you think that's any of her business?" Pamela asked, her cornflower blue eyes wide and seemingly innocent.

"Just a second," Dana cut in, trying to keep her tone even and unhurried. "I never said anything like that."

"Let's let Pamela finish, shall we?" Ms. Allardyce said.

"It's just that it was my understanding that guidance counselors weren't allowed to tell anyone anything," Pamela said, folding her hands neatly in front of her.

"What was the date of your appointment, Pamela?" Michael interjected, his deep voice steady and penetrating.

"What? Which one?" Pamela looked a little flustered.

"The first one. First time you and I met."

"Well, I can't remember. I really don't know."

Michael produced a small black book from the inside pocket of his camel corduroy jacket. "It was three weeks ago Tuesday. I always write down my appointments. Now, Dana, when did you mention Pamela to me?"

"I . . . I don't know." She wanted desperately to say that she'd never mentioned her at all, but she'd promised Faith and Shelley that she would tell the truth. "But I never would have brought up her name if she hadn't begged me to. She said she was failing, and she was frightened. I'd already seen you twice, and she was nervous about her first appointment. She said you had the last word on expelling kids. Also, she knew

that if she failed any of her midterms, she'd
be docked from the midwinter dance, which
she was," Dana added, turning to Ms. Allardyce with a look of complete candor on her
face. "I didn't really know anything about her
grades, honest. But she seemed so scared
about the whole thing, and she made me
believe I could help by telling Michael she
was really trying. So *I* brought her name up,
but he didn't answer — he just changed the
subject. And I had no idea what I was doing
was illegal." Dana gulped, swallowing back
tears. She would have liked to tell Ms. Allardyce how wouderful he was, how invaluable to the school, but that was beside the
point right now.

"All right, then. Dana, you and I had seen
each other that Monday, the day before
I first saw Pamela." He pointed down at his
notebook, and then got up to hand it to Ms.
Allardyce. "I didn't know what her situation
was at that point, because I only had the
transcript of her grades, and a few notes
from some of her teachers. It would have
been virtually impossible to talk about a girl
I'd never met, *if* I did things like that. Dana
mentioned Pamela to me the following Monday, at which point I'd seen and heard enough
to make up my own mind. I didn't respond
when she mentioned Pamela's name, and she
never brought her up again. You'll see here,
Ms. Allardyce, that I always write down the
content of my sessions in my own shorthand.

The initials P.Y. are recorded in that Monday's entry. Dana, have I ever mentioned another student to you in our sessions?"

"*Never*." Dana said the word as emphatically as she could.

Michael walked over to Pamela and stood, towering over her. "What disturbs me is your methods, Pamela. If you truly thought I was doing anything to betray your trust, you should have mentioned it to me directly. But you *knew* I hadn't, and you were angry at me because I was partially responsible for any decisions made about your future here. You wanted to get back at me. I think you and I have a lot of talking to do in the future."

"But, I . . . Ms. Allardyce, this isn't fair," Pamela whined.

"What isn't, Pamela? I must say, in situations like this, it's generally one person's word against another. But Mr. Frank has facts and figures, and all you have is suppositions. If Dana hadn't come right out and said that she brought up your name, we would have had no way of proving anything, would we? You didn't think this one out too well, dear, did you?" Ms. Allardyce smiled over at Michael and said softly. "I think counseling is in order. Deal with it as you see fit."

Dana was suddenly aware that she hadn't taken a breath for the past couple of moments. She gasped with relief, and everyone

looked over at her. "I'm really sorry. This
was mostly my fault."

"No, Dana," Michael said bluntly. "It was
Pamela's fault. Never take the rap for someone else, kid," he added in an undertone.
"You've got nothing to gain by it. "Well,"
he said, walking briskly to the door, "I don't
think we should take up any more of Ms.
Allardyce's time." He held the living room
door open, and Dana came to his side at
once, surprised by his toughness with Pamela but very glad of the outcome. The other
girl, her head down, straggled across the
room, almost reluctant to leave.

"I'd like to see you in my office at lunchtime tomorrow," Michael told her bluntly.
"And I'll tell you right now that no excuses
will be acceptable."

Pamela scowled at him, and for a moment,
Dana thought she was going to refuse. Then
she shrugged. "You can talk my ear off; it
won't do a bit of good. Ms. Allardyce, my
mother will hear about this."

"I've already got a call in to California so
I can tell her myself, dear," the headmistress
said with an odd little smile. "I advise you to
pay attention to Mr. Frank. He can do you
a great deal of good, if you let him. Thank
you all for coming," she said politely as
Michael ushered the two girls out and closed
the door behind them.

Pamela grabbed her cape and stormed
out, racing down the path and out of sight.

Michael and Dana watched until they couldn't see her anymore. Then, as though by a prearranged signal, they both started walking slowly back toward the library.

"I know I'm not supposed to talk to you about her," Dana said, "but I just want to tell you how glad I am that somebody finally met her on her own terms and got the best of her. And how happy I am that you didn't get into any trouble," she added shyly. "I never would have forgiven myself if you had."

"You coming to dinner tonight?" Michael asked cheerily, as if she hadn't spoken. "Shelley's dong very well, I hear."

"Very well." *Better than me, actually,* Dana thought, as she nodded yes. She longed to tell him how she felt, but the words stuck in her mouth.

"Terrific. Wait'll you taste my home cooking," he grinned. "Bring your own Coke, if you want it," he told her. "I don't stock it anymore. See you." And then he was off, jogging ahead of her. For once, she felt like she couldn't keep up.

For the next two hours, she regaled Faith and Shelley with tales of The Allardyce Inquisition, as she called it. She didn't tell them how her heart was pounding when she walked back down the path with Michael, nor how much she dreaded this dinner tonight. It was one thing to care so terribly about someone that it hurt, and it was an-

other to keep it on an even keel, to act as
though it were the most normal thing in the
world to be walking on air one minute and
slogging down in the depths the next.

At six-thirty, the girls bundled up and
made their way through the maple grove
to the faculty houses. Michael's front windows were all lit up, and they could see Alison stirring something in a pot on the kitchen
stove. Faith and Shelley looked at Dana,
whose face was an utter blank.

"It'll probably be delicious," Shelley assured her as they rang the bell.

"It's got to be better than R.B. with N.G.,"
Faith added.

"Well, good evening!" Michael's manner
was jovial as he greeted them and took their
coats. "Welcome to the first healthy dinner
party of the season. Once this catches on,
everybody's going to be doing it, but remember, we started it."

Dana had never seen Alison so effusive,
so glowing. Her hair shone in the light of
the candles that illuminated the oak table,
and she looked positively radiant as she
poured tea into lovely Japanese cups and
turned up the heat under the vegetable
casserole. She chatted away as though she
really belonged here, in this house, which
depressed Dana terribly.

The other girls pretended not to notice as
Alison and Michael served, and Shelley began rattling on about her French class that

morning. Everyone seemed to be trying extra hard to cheer Dana up, even though the occasion had been planned on Shelley's behalf.

Dana wanted nothing more than to leave, to not have to see the obvious affection between Michael and Alison.

The telephone buzzed gently in the next room, and Michael excused himself as he went in to answer it. There was a brief silence at the table as Faith and Shelley looked over at Dana and saw the tight expression on her face. Alison clearly noticed it, too.

"I have this terrible feeling that I'm spoiling Doby rotten," she interjected, crossing one chopstick over the other on the edge of her plate. To make the meal even more unusual, everyone was eating it with chopsticks. It took a little longer, but it was a lot more fun. "That cat is becoming impossible," she continued. "He won't eat his nice cat food anymore, not since I fed him that curried rice the other day. I don't know what to do."

"Dana, it's a long-distance call for you," Michael said from the doorway. "The switchboard transferred it over here. You can take it in the living room."

She frowned and got up, grateful only for the chance to remove herself from the company. Her hand accidentally brushed Michael's as she walked past him, and for some reason, it made her want to cry.

"Hello?" she said into the receiver.

"Hi, honey!" Her father's voice was suddenly in the room with her, very close and comforting.

"Dad! I can't wait to see you," she smiled.

"Just wanted to let you know that our plane's coming in Friday morning. If you take the train down after your last class, we'll meet you at Grand Central. Then we'll have the whole weekend to talk."

"Great. I'll be there," she promised.

"Eve sends her love, baby. She's bringing you a genuine Hawaiian lei. This particular variety is supposed to bring you lots of luck in love."

Dana licked her lips, which were suddenly very dry. "Wonderful. I'll wear it all the time."

"See you then, sweetie. Stay warm."

"Bye, Dad." But as she hung up, she felt frosty. It was a good thing she was going home this weekend, she thought as she walked back into Michael's kitchen. There was no way she could stick around here.

CHAPTER ELEVEN

New York looked sparkling and cold in the brief glimpse Dana had of it before the train entered the long tunnel. But she scarcely noticed the streets and lights, because she was so excited about seeing her family — both halves of it — and she did love this city, in every season. There was something about Manhattan that refreshed and excited her.

She saw them as soon as she started walking up the ramp. John Morrison was wearing his double-breasted trench coat and looked very much like a handsome spy. He was tanned and smiling. Eve was standing beside him, her orange-yellow hair nearly matching the high boots she was wearing. Eve always looked like a picture out of a fashion magazine, Dana thought with just a whiff of envy. The only thing she still couldn't get used to was how much younger Eve was than her father. Why, Eve was just about Alison's age, maybe a couple of years older.

"Darling, you look wonderful!" Her father raced toward her and gathered her up in his arms. They hugged for a long moment, and Dana closed her eyes as she drew in John Morrison's wonderful presence. How she'd missed him! She hadn't really realized it until just this minute.

"We're so glad to see you!" Eve stuck her head between them and gave Dana a peck on the cheek. Dana reciprocated, a little less warmly. She still didn't really know how to behave around her stepmother. Or rather, around her father's wife. Stepmothers only came about when they had custody, along with your father. That certainly wasn't the case here.

"Are you hungry? Where shall we go?" John Morrison asked, steering Eve and Dana out into the crowded station.

It was kind of tradition for Dana and her mother and Maggie to go to the deli right near their apartment house when Dana came home for a weekend. She didn't mention it, of course. She couldn't go there with Eve.

"Oh, anyplace. I'm not that hungry, really."

"Then we'll take you back to our hotel. The dining room's good, and you can get a light bite. You're, ah, sure you don't want to stay with us? We can still get you a room," her father said hesitantly.

"Mom and Maggie are expecting me," Dana pointed out. She looked at Eve out of the corner of her eye, and the comparison with Alison struck her again. Of course, they looked nothing alike, but there was a similarity of attitude. They were both so self-assured, like they knew what they wanted out of life. Dana wished that she did.

They took a cab uptown, through midtown and past the fancy Madison Avenue shops to the Westbury, an elegant but comfortable hotel frequented, John Morrison said, by visiting diplomats. Dana's eyes devoured the busy streets, the wonderful mannequins wearing outlandish clothing in every store, the towering architecture that spelled NEW YORK in capital letters. She was so busy looking around, she hardly heard her father and Eve chatting away about what they'd been doing lately in Hawaii.

"Okay, climb out," Mr. Morrison said as the cab pulled to a screeching halt in front of the hotel. Dana and Eve walked into the lobby and waited for him to pay the driver.

"How's school?" Eve asked as they stood there together. She was sizing Dana up, her keen eyes trying to perceive the feelings underneath the facade.

"Fine. Busy," Dana said noncommittally. She wondered what Michael would make of this young woman her father was so in love with. She wondered what Michael was doing, right at that very moment. She wondered whether he thought about her at all when he wasn't with her, the way she did about him.

"All right, ladies." John Morrison ushered the two of them through the lobby to the dining room. "Table for three, please," he told the maître d'. With a great flourish, the man showed them to a place in the corner, a lovely banquette with a spray of spring flowers and a candle on the table.

"Now." Dana's father settled back and stared at his daughter. "How's my baby?"

Dana shook a warning finger at him. "I'm not the baby, Dad."

"She's right there, John." Eve gave him a wink.

"Anyhow, I'm fine," Dana continued as the waiter came over to take their order. "Could I have a grilled cheese and tomato?" she asked. "And an orange soda, please?"

"Sure you don't want something fancier?" her father asked. "After all, we're celebrating."

"Oh? No, thanks," Dana said, immediately on her guard. "I just want a sandwich."

"And two steaks, please," her father told the waiter. "Medium rare. Perrier for the lady, and a glass of red wine for me."

Dana noticed that he'd ordered for Eve. How did he know what she wanted, Dana thought somewhat angrily. Or was that what happened after you'd been married for a few months? Suddenly, you give up your own personality and let someone else take charge. *Well, that'll never happen to me,* she vowed, watching Eve place her elegant, small hand over her father's large one. Unless it was more like what went on between her and Michael when they thought the same thought at the same moment. Yes, that was certainly possible — and preferable, Dana decided.

"So we wrapped up the last account early," her father was saying. "And we just hope the rest of them go as well."

"How many more do you have to do?" Dana asked, probing for the special news. "Will you still be finished by the end of the year?"

"Looks that way," Eve smiled. "But maybe we'll stay on for the summer, just laze around the beach for a month or so. How about it, Dana? Would you come out for a visit?"

Right after her father and Eve had married, last June, they'd asked if she wanted to come to Hawaii with them for the year. It was certainly tempting, but she'd said no at the last minute. She simply couldn't leave Canby Hall, and living without Faith and Shelley seemed more than she could bear. But a month in the summer . . . and if he *really* was coming back at the end of the year. But she had to know — she just couldn't be cool and calm another minute.

"What were you going to tell me, Dad?" she asked determinedly, ignoring Eve's invitation. "I want to know the special news first."

"Well . . ." Her father reached over and put his arm around Eve. "I'm glad you asked, because it's hard to keep something like this under your hat. Darling, we have the pleasure of announcing that next July, you are going to have a little brother or sister. What do you think of that?" He turned to give Eve a quick kiss on the lips.

Dana felt paralyzed. "A . . . baby? You're pregnant?"

Eve nodded vehemently. "Yes."

"Well, that's . . . I'm really happy for you. Really." She wanted to be, more than anything; she wanted to feel the joy that the two of them shared, but something in her hung back, waiting on the sidelines. "I'm just so amazed, that's all," she said to explain her sudden silence. "Congratulations, both of you." She took her father's hand and squeezed it, then kissed Eve.

"You remember how I told you I came from this huge family with cousins absolutely everywhere?" Eve said as the waiter returned with their meals. "Well, John and I decided it was time to start a branch of our own. But you and Maggie are our family, too — you know that, don't you, Dana?"

"Oh, yes, of course." There was a big lump at the back of her throat. She took a sip of soda, but it refused to go away. And once again, as she had with Shelley, she felt mean and petty and selfish. Who was she to spoil their wonderful news?

"Does Maggie. . . ? Have you told her yet?"

"We picked her up at school today. She's walking on air. Apparently, she's taking a home-ec child care course, and she's become the class diapering ace. Says she can't wait to try out her skills on our little one." Eve grinned. "She probably knows more than I do about babies at this point."

"Don't worry, Eve." John Morrison gave his wife a hug. "I have experience — I'll show you the ropes."

The rest of the meal was filled with laughter and jokes (theirs) and a great deal of solemn thought (Dana's). When the check came, Eve tactfully made her excuses so that Dana and her father could be alone for a while.

"He'll take you home, if that's okay. I still have jet lag, and I think the pregnancy doesn't help," she said lightly. "We got theater tickets for you and Maggie tomorrow. A matinee of New York's hottest musical — how about that? Good-night, sweetie — see you in the morning." She kissed Dana again, and then she was gone.

John Morrison paid and swept Dana outside, where the doorman hailed them a cab. They got in and snuggled together, and for some reason, Dana thought of those nights long ago, when her father used to tuck her in and then put his cheek next to hers on the pillow. The remembrance made her unaccountably sad.

"So what do you think?" he asked, as she knew he would.

"About the baby?"

He nodded.

"I didn't know you wanted to start all over again with diapers and formula," she laughed nervously. Then she looked up at him, knowing she couldn't lie. "I'm a little surprised, I guess. That's all. You know I'm happy for you."

"I thought this would be hard on you, Dana. On you more than Maggie. You're the sensitive one."

"Yeah," she laughed, thinking of all she'd been through lately. "You could call it that."

The cab drove up Park and Dana was smiling again. "Just give me some time to get used to it, will you? I have to start thinking of you as the one who's going to give out cigars in a few months instead of my dad — mine and Maggie's."

"I'll always be that, sweetie. First and foremost."

But you'll never be coming home again. You'll never marry my mother again, the way I hoped you would, she thought in a moment of self-pity. Then she took a breath and leaned over to plant a kiss on his tanned cheek. "It's okay — really it is," she whispered as the cab pulled up in front of her apartment house.

"See you tomorrow, baby. Be at the hotel about noon, okay? And tell Maggie to wear something that's not jeans. Love ya."

The cab pulled away so fast, she scarcely managed to get a last look at his face. She wasn't sure, but she thought he looked worried about her.

"Well, look who's here!" Smitty, the doorman, was clearly pleased to see Dana. "I was just asking your mother about you yesterday."

"It's nice to be here," she smiled, "even just for the weekend." She walked through the lobby, relishing the old familiar smell, the leather chairs, the creaking of the elevator as it came to a halt on the first floor. "Would you call upstairs to let them know I'm coming, Smitty?" she asked the doorman as she climbed into the car.

On her way upstairs, she practiced reacting. "Well, so they're having a baby — can you believe it! Isn't it marvelous! Eve is positively glowing. It's wonderful, don't you think?"

"Darling! Welcome home!" Her mother was waiting at the elevator, and as it opened, she caught her daughter in the act of talking to the thin air. "Don't tell me — the house is haunted!" Carol Morrison, dressed impeccably as usual in a khaki cotton jumpsuit and a maroon scarf, peered into the elevator and scoured it for ghosts. "I can't see any — phooey."

"Hi, Mom." Dana smiled sheepishly, putting down her duffel bag to give her mother a big kiss. Her sister Maggie appeared in the doorway of their apartment, and as she opened the door, a blast of the Stones buffeted the hallway.

"Close that door! The neighbors are going to throw us out if you keep that up," Carol Morrison chided as she whisked both her daughters into the apartment. "Can you turn that down, dear, just long enough to say hi to your sister?"

"Hi, you boarding school person, you!" Maggie's elfin face turned into an enormous smile as she hugged Dana around the waist and spun her in a circle in time to the music.

It was hard to feel down when you looked at Maggie. Her good humor and silliness were infectious.

"Anybody want popcorn?" The girls' mother made a beeline for the kitchen. "I have an unreasonable desire to make some noise of my own. I think the popper will do it." She whizzed out of the room, leaving the girls alone in the cream-and-aqua living room.

"How's everything?" Maggie yelled above the percussion.

"Great! Hey, it's like a disco in here." Dana

grinned at her sister, wondering at the differences between them. She'd never been like that at Maggie's age, she thought. She was more the country-music-moanin'-low type anyway. "Could we just lower it about sixty decibels?" she shrieked at precisely the moment when Mick Jagger decided to call it quits. The room was deafeningly quiet.

"I can't believe it," their mother called from the kitchen.

"Oh, Mom!" said Maggie. She took her sister by the hand and sat her on the sofa. "D'you hear their news?"

Dana nodded. "I hear you're real excited."

"Who wouldn't be?" Maggie tucked her feet up under her knees and sighed. "Kind of incredible." Then she noticed the expression on Dana's face. "What'sa matter?"

"Oh, I don't know. I don't mean to be a party pooper. It'll just take me a day or so for it to sink in. Does Mom know?" she asked in an undertone.

"Sure, sure." Carol Morrison appeared in the kitchen doorway holding a spatula. "Oh, well, more power to them, I say. I wouldn't go through that baby route again if you paid me. Well, let me amend that. Maybe I would if you paid me a *lot*." With that, she disappeared into the kitchen.

"What a Mom, huh?" Maggie whispered. "She's putting up a brave front."

Dana's heart went out to her mother.

"Don't look like that," Maggie said in a softer voice. "Babies are nice — you'll see."

"I know they are, silly," Dana laughed. "We were babies once ourselves."

"Please, don't remind me!" Carol Morrison raced back into the room with the popper, which was going like crazy. "Yikes — I can't keep the lid on!" The thing exploded, little puff-balls of white corn jumping all over the room. The three of them, laughing hysterically, got down on their hands and knees to gather up the wild escapees. Then they sat up and talked till all hours, and it wasn't until she went to bed much later that Dana remembered how she felt.

The word was lonely.

CHAPTER TWELVE

Dana got back on Sunday right after dinner. She'd had a long time on the train — four and a half hours to be exact — to consider just what had happened this weekend. The thing was, the more she thought about it, the more confused she became. Sometimes the picture looked bleak; then the sky would clear and she would decide that it might not be so bad to be a kind of sister-aunt to a little newborn.

Maybe just a few more hours to think it over would do the trick, she decided as she slogged into Baker. As she walked in, everyone was scurrying to Study Hours. At Canby Hall, every night except Saturday from seven-thirty to nine-thirty was relegated to cracking the books. Sunday was particularly frenetic as girls tried to make up all the homework they'd neglected during the week and over the weekend. Tonight, Dana wanted nothing more than to curl up on her bed with a good book — or even a dull one.

She hurried inside Baker and took the stairs two at a time. There was so much to tell Faith and Shelley, she didn't know where to begin. And there was Song Night tonight — she didn't want to miss that.

Before she could do anything, however, she had to sign in on the bulletin board outside Alison's apartment and stick her head in the door to say hello. This was ostensibly so that the housemother always knew that everyone who'd signed out on Friday was back at school, but it was really so that Alison could have some private time with each girl once in a while. The returning students were supposed to go in for a little tea and sympathy. As Dana made her way up the stairs, she wondered if there was a way out of this. She didn't feel very sympathetic toward Alison right now.

She put down her duffel bag, signed her name on the check sheet, and tapped on the door.

"C'mon in," came the familiar call.

Dana hesitated, then pushed open the door. "I'm back from New York," she said.

Alison was seated in the comfortable chair she'd wedged under the pipes of the penthouse room. Alison had painted each one a different primary color, and, seated there smiling, with Doby curled up in her lap, she looked very much like the Cheshire Cat, waiting for visitors. To Dana's surprise, the housemother was wearing her horn-rimmed glasses.

"What happened to your contacts?" Dana asked without stepping into the room. Alison didn't get up.

"Oh," she said with an embarrassed laugh. "It's Sunday, you know. Thought I'd give them a rest."

There was a long, awkward pause. Then Alison bolted out of her chair, sending the cat sprawling to the floor.

"Ah . . . would you like some tea?" This was another part of the tradition. Alison would make the girls herb tea and serve them high-nutrition protein cookies while they poured out their problems to her.

"I don't think so, thanks," Dana said, shifting from foot to foot. "I've got a long history chapter to read before tomorrow."

"Oh, okay."

Dana could scarcely believe her ears. Alison *never* agreed with ducking out. If anything, she'd figure something was really wrong with any girl who didn't want the Sunday night rap session and insist she stay. Not tonight; not Dana.

"Well, so . . . I'll see you at Song Night then," Dana muttered, picking up her duffel.

"Right. Thanks for coming by," Alison said needlessly. It was funny, really, Dana mused as she raced down the stairs to Room 407. Alison felt awkward around her. In a way, that was very flattering. She wasn't treating Dana like a silly little girl but rather, as serious competition. Because why else would Alison act that way? If it weren't for Michael, she would have been her old, casual, easy self.

"Yay! You're back!" Shelley yelled as Dana opened the door of their room.

"About time, too," Faith sighed from her unusual upside-down position. She let herself down slowly from the shoulder-stand and sat crosslegged on her mat, grinning at Dana. "We're champing at the bit for the big news."

"How's your dad?" Shelley asked. "And your mom?" It was hard for Shelley to think of parents as separate units. Before Dana, she'd never been very friendly with a divorced kid before. Of course, before Faith, she'd never known anyone who wasn't white. Divorce still seemed the more foreign to her.

"Well, hold onto your hats, guys." Dana sat heavily on her bed. She looked at Faith, then at Shelley, and then she took a deep breath and told them.

"But . . . but isn't he a little *old* for that?" Shelley demanded. "He must be older than everyone we know combined."

"It's not the *man's* age that counts, you dummy," Faith laughed. "My grandfather was sixty when he had his last son. Did I ever tell you I was two years older than my Uncle Archer?"

"You're kidding!" Dana was fascinated.

"Well, are you happy?" Shelley asked as the conversation kind of sat there.

"Truth?"

"Truth," they both chorused.

"Not really. Of course, I didn't tell him that. Maggie is delirious, so that should make up for my lack of enthusiasm. I just can't imagine him starting all over again, you know? I thought Mag and I were enough."

"Maybe it's not that," Faith said, coming over to put an arm around Dana. "Maybe they just want something that's all their own, not part of any other family. There'll be enough love to go round — there always is."

"Ooh, you're so wise!" Dana picked up a pillow and threw it at Faith. "How did you get to be so all-fired smart, huh?"

"It runs in my family." Faith grinned. "Now what say we get going to Song Night? Sounds to me like you've got some loud music to make tonight." She picked up her roommates' parkas, grabbed Dana's guitar from its peg on the wall, and raced them to the door. Dana followed her, then looked back at Shelley, who was still sitting at her desk, her arms folded.

"Yes?" Dana inquired.

"I was just thinking, I bet you can use this experience in some way. You know, the way a great actress uses things from real life in her characters on stage." The dramatic Shelley, who surfaced every once in a while, was speaking now. When she saw the look on Dana's face, she shrugged sheepishly. "Okay, I give, it's lousy. Just plain lousy. Let's go sing."

Song Night had traditionally been a once-yearly affair with everyone sitting around the auditorium stage, accompanied by a couple of guitars and a piano. For the past year, the event had been upgraded, since everyone seemed to enjoy it so much. Now, the girls called one every month or so. Michael had offered his office as the new location, because it was clearly more cozy than the auditorium.

By the time Faith, Shelley, and Dana got to the library, the conference room was nearly full, and they had to wedge their way in along the back wall. Michael and Alison were standing beside a couple of seniors near the front, getting ready to call everyone to attention.

"Could we have our guitars front and center, please? Dana? Nancy? Cheryl? Come on up here." Michael steered them into position.

Dana looked at him, relishing his closeness. She was happy to be here, beside him. After all, they'd been apart for the whole weekend, and she'd missed him.

"How're you doing?" he asked her casually.

"Later," she whispered. Then, thinking

better of it, she asked, "Can I see you to-morrow?"

He nodded, seemingly busy getting two freshmen seated. "Four o'clock. I'll be here."

She took her seat in the center of the circle beside the other two guitarists. Then she nodded at Nancy, and on the downbeat, they launched into "Michael, Row Your Boat Ashore." It was kind of corny, but everyone knew it, so it was a good song to start with because it got the kids involved at once.

Cheryl led in next with a Beatles medley, and the group got rowdier, clapping and swaying to the beat. They quieted down a bit for the slow numbers, but there was one voice that always stood out. Michael's deep baritone rose over the other sounds, adding a low, rumbling accompaniment. He had a warm voice, just like his personality. It didn't matter at all to Dana that he was never on key. Of course, she thought with a grin as Nancy struck up the first notes of "Greensleeves," there wasn't much he did that bothered her.

"Wait a sec." Alison clapped her hands to get the group's attention. "Let's have a little school spirit here before we close. Our alma mater, please." Then they all stood and sang the rousing melody. The last notes died away slowly, and then the girls closest to the door began to leave.

Dana turned to say good-night to Michael,

but he wasn't looking in her direction. That was all right, she thought as she hurried over to join her roommates. Tomorrow they'd have plenty of time to talk. And finally, she knew what had to be said.

He was waiting for her at four o'clock, seated on the floor of his office surrounded by stacks of file folders. He looked up, startled, when she knocked on the open door.

"Oh, Dana! Please, come in and rescue me from this paperwork. I'm drowning in it," he complained, scooping everything into one pile and shoving it aside. "Life would be great if there weren't all these forms to fill out."

"Um," she said. He looked so wonderful today, in a starchy white shirt open at the collar and charcoal gray slacks.

"So, what can I do for you?" he asked, leaning back against the large pillow that was propped up beside him.

She walked to the window and stared out at the glistening, white park. Long icicles hung from every tree branch, making a brilliant landscape even brighter. Dana cleared her throat, gathering her thoughts. She was finally through beating around the bush. Or at least she would be after just a slight push to get her started.

"You went home this weekend, didn't you?" he said when she was silent. "Saw your father and his wife?"

"You remembered." She smiled gratefully.

"That's my job, ma'am."

"Well. . . ." She paused, then walked across to the next bank of pillows where she took a seat. "It all came clear to me. Remember when I first came to see you and you asked what was the matter and I didn't know?"

He nodded, his kind eyes holding her in their embrace.

"I know now. I knew on Friday night when my father told me they were having a baby — he and his wife."

Michael frowned and crossed his arms. "Pretty heavy."

"Yes, but it's not as bad as I thought, really. I mean, that's their thing — not mine. It doesn't have a lot to do with me. But when he broke the news, it reminded me of when I was a kid, when the bigger kids in the park were choosing up teams and I was too little to play. 'Come back when you're quart-size, pint-size,' they said. I was so . . . lonely. So left out."

"And you're left out again now." It was a statement, not a question. For some reason, his extreme surety made her angry.

"You're big enough to play on that team now, Dana," Michael said. "Which means you get to take your lumps along with the rest of us."

She got up, overwhelmed with the emotions that filled her and spilled out of her.

"Why don't you tell me all of it before you

bust a blood vessel holding it in," he suggested quietly.

She nodded grudgingly. "Sometimes, I don't like myself a whole lot. Like my really bad feelings about Pamela or when I didn't know about Shelley. . . ." She bit her lip. "Sorry, I shouldn't be talking about them."

"It's okay. Look, Pamela is water under the bridge, and as for Shelley, she's taken care of that. And if it makes you feel any better, no one knew about her."

"That's true." Dana walked back to the window, and turned to lean on the sill. She was very close to him. "But why should I feel like this? I have Shelley and Faith and Mom and Maggie and so many great friends here at school. And even Randy. . . ." She stopped, not wanting to think too much about him right now. "And you," she stammered.

"I'm here," he nodded.

She let out her breath. "Oh, Michael, I love you!" She heard the words she'd said and looked down at him, horrified. This was terrible! She hadn't ever meant to say that to him. It was for her, alone, to know.

But his face hadn't changed. It didn't look pleased or sorry, and that made her feel worse.

"I mean. . . ." But there was no way to retract that statement. She had opened Pandora's box, and all the gremlins were out, dancing around and having a ball at her expense. "I have to get out of here," she blurted, stumbling toward the door, her cheeks aflame. She ran, grabbing her parka, not even bothering to put it on until she was out in the air and realized that she was cold.

I'll never be able to look him in the eye again, she thought miserably. *Oh, how could I have been so dumb!* Her only consolation, if you could call it that, was that she had told the truth.

CHAPTER THIRTEEN

The odd thing was, she felt better after that. Well, not happy, of course — she was completely mortified — but she'd gotten the worst of it off her chest.

Love. What was that, anyway? She'd been in love with Bret Harper for a while, and she felt a certain love for Randy that was mixed with deep friendship. But this was the first time she ever *loved* someone who wasn't her family. It was a wonderful, awful feeling, akin to that high dive you take into a deep, icy lake on a magical spring night. You know it's going to shock you, but the thrill of being there is worth it.

She knew nothing would ever be the same between her and Michael, and much as that saddened her, she guessed it was all for the best. If she had lost his respect, at least she had given herself a little peace.

Faith and Shelley noticed it, too. They

didn't ask what had happened, but they knew that something was different about Dana. As if she had passed through a difficult obstacle course and come out on the other side, exhausted but conquering. For the first time in months, they could stop tiptoeing around her. She'd almost come back to the world of the living.

"So where's Randy these days?" Faith asked casually the following Sunday afternoon. They'd had a brief thaw in the weather, and everything was dripping.

"Hmm?" Dana switched off her Walkman and pushed her headphones back on her head. "Not sure."

Shelley gave Faith a look. "He hasn't disappeared or anything, has he? Hasn't ridden off into the sunset?"

Dana frowned. "I don't think so. Why?"

"Because I know you didn't think your match was made in heaven, but he's a good guy. I'm hoping you haven't given up on him for some stupid reason." Shelley got up and walked over to her, so she had to look her in the eye.

"You know we haven't been dating regularly for a while," Dana explained patiently. "And I was pretty awful to him a couple of weeks ago. I guess, if I were him, I wouldn't call me either."

"Then why don't you pick up the phone yourself, girl?" Faith demanded.

"What is this? Why are the two of you ganging up on me?" Dana sat up, annoyed at them, and at herself. She *had* been meaning to call Randy. She just hadn't gotten around to it.

"You can't go on like this, you know," Faith said sternly. "You've got to wake up to what's happening here. Sorry to be a bully, Dana, but you've got it coming. And finally, you can take it."

Dana shook her head, glancing from one roommate to the other. "Well, what?" she asked, more than a little curious.

Neither Shelley nor Faith really wanted this confrontation. They just felt they owed it to her. "All right," Faith began, "but let's do it walking. I always think better walking." She put on her parka and waited. Finally, Dana shrugged and followed suit.

"How about the old elm out by the skating pond?" Shelley suggested. "That's good thinking territory."

"You two are really pushing it," Dana complained. But she went willingly, past Addison House and out toward the old Canby Hall where the original buildings and grounds of the estate had been. They passed the chapel and finally came to the skating pond. The ice was too slushy today — no one was out there.

"Now," Dana persisted. "Will you get to the point?"

Faith nodded. "I'm ready. Dana, we care about you, and we don't ever like to see you hurting. But . . . sometimes, you take things too seriously, you know?"

"I know," Dana sighed. "So what else is new?"

"You're the big, sophisticated New York City girl, right? You ought to have learned to keep some perspective from that creep, Bret Harper."

"How do you mean?"

"When he was keeping you on a string," Shelley continued, "and you kept insisting that he'd reformed and was a one-woman man. Well, you finally saw the light. It wasn't like that."

"And you kept your sense of humor," Faith added.

"Not all the time," Dana confessed.

"But look at you *now*, Dana," Shelley said softly. "This time you're not laughing."

Dana licked her lips and nodded. "You're right. But it's over now," she said softly.

"It is," Faith said. "But it's not. If it were over, you'd call Randy."

"They have nothing to do with each other," Dana protested. She hadn't mentioned *his* name and didn't intend to, or need to.

Shelley did it for her. "Of course they do. You have to let go of Michael first," she said.

"I'm not holding on to him," Dana laughed, but her laugh had no humor in it.

"Aren't you? Look, Michael's a logical choice for you, somebody you of all people would like. He's a listener.

"But you have to understand," Faith went on, putting her mittened hand on Dana's shoulder. "Michael's a grown-up. He needs a woman, not a teen-ager. I mean, I know he likes you and all that, but what you really want from him could never be."

"Don't be silly. I *never* thought of Michael that way." She tried to deny it.

"And then there's Alison," Faith said. "He's fallen for her. Admit it."

And there was the final barrier. It wasn't enough for her to have decided never to darken his door again, not enough that she'd had to give him up in one stupid sweep of emotion. Now, she had let him fall in love with someone else. That was too cruel. Unfortunately, Faith and Shelley were right.

"I'll call Randy," was all she said. But they knew there was a lot more than that going on inside her.

She didn't call him. She couldn't. Something as important as this had to be taken care of in person. As far back as Dana could remember, most of the misunderstandings of her life had happened over the telephone.

Margaret, the cook, lived out near the Crowell farm, she recalled. After lunch, she went around to the kitchen and waved.

"Are you driving home this afternoon?" Dana asked her. "Could you give me a lift?"

"Why, of course, dear. Just let me grab my coat." Margaret was glad for the company, and chattered most of the way. Dana listened politely, but her mind was elsewhere. In a way, she was looking forward to seeing the look on his face. And in another way, she was terrified that she might be letting herself in for yet another humiliation. Suppose he told her to get lost?

They slowed down as they approached the Crowell farm, which was one of the largest in the area. "This where you said you wanted me to leave you?" Margaret asked, as they saw the signboard advertising fresh cider and eggs.

"That's great, Margaret, anywhere along here," Dana said, excited now. She saw Randy and Bob moving along the split-rail fence together, looking for holes. Bob was one of Randy's five brothers, and the one who looked most like him.

"What time you want me to come by for you, dear?" Margaret asked. "I got to start dinner about four-thirty."

"That's okay." Dana smiled as she opened the door on the passenger side and climbed out. "I'll get back by myself." She jerked her head in the boys' direction. Was this wishful thinking? If Randy refused to speak to her, she was going to have an awfully long walk

back to school. Still, she'd been burning a
lot of bridges lately, so she might as well
torch one more.

"See you later, then. Have fun!" Margaret
waved as she pulled away.

The boys looked up at the sound of the
departing car. Dana saw Randy squint into
the sun, then frown. He said a few words to
Bob, who nodded understandingly. Dana
started to walk toward them, her heart doing
about fifty miles per hour.

"Hello!" she said cheerily when she was
a few yards away. She tried to make her
voice casual, as if she popped up unexpect-
edly every other day or so.

"Hi there, Dana," Bob said, picking up his
bale of fence wire and wire cutters. "Sorry
I can't stick around, but I promised I'd run
into town for Dad." He nodded to her, then
strolled away. Randy still hadn't said a word,
but that wasn't unusual for Randy.

She walked over to him and leaned
against the fence, looking into his clear
gray eyes. "I came to mend some fences of
my own," she said quietly.

"I knew it." Randy shrugged and went
back to work.

"Did you?" She was a little miffed that he
was taking this as though it were his due.

"I knew that once you had your fill of all
that privacy you were craving, you'd need to
talk about it to somebody. I never met a girl

who likes to talk so much." His etched features broadened into a grin, and then he threw down his tools and opened his arms to her. "Wish you'd talk my ear off," he whispered as he gently cupped her chin in his hand and brought her face close to his. "But not just yet," he said. Then, very softly, he kissed her.

She relished the feel of his lips on hers, the way they just stood there together, sheltering each other from the cold. An enormous calm came over her, a sense of belonging, of fitting in.

"Randy," she said when at last they broke apart. "I was totally rotten to you. I don't know what got into me, but it won't happen again — I promise."

"That's good." He took her at her word, and didn't question it. She would have liked to explain everything, from start to finish, but that just wasn't his style. For once, she let it be.

They spent the afternoon together. She watched him work with the horses, start up the cider press, joke with his brothers. She helped him collect eggs from the small henhouse and then watched the football game with him. It was a lovely afternoon, and Dana's only regret was that she'd deprived herself of so many others like this because of her own weirdness.

It would have been perfect if she hadn't

thought about Michael on the ride home. She supposed, though, as she forced him out of her mind, that he'd be showing up there a lot for the next few weeks, or even months. She wasn't going to stop loving him, just like that. The only way to get rid of him completely would be to avoid him as much as possible around school. That was the only way she'd ever recover. And it wasn't as though she were going back to Randy on the rebound — not at all. She cared about him in a very real way. There was no reason to feel guilty because he wasn't the only person she cared about.

"I'll talk to you soon, okay?" Randy said as he pulled the pickup truck around the front of Baker.

"Very soon," she agreed with a smile. Then she grabbed the lapels of his sheepskin jacket and pulled him close for a kiss.

"I've missed you," he said in a rare moment of self-revelation. "Nice to have you back, Dana."

She climbed down and watched him drive away, and felt perfectly wonderful until she walked inside Baker. She was on her way up the stairs when Alison called down to her over the banister.

"Dana, could you come up here and help me, please? I'm trying to move this plant and it's fighting back."

"Sure," Dana said, trudging up toward the

penthouse. She noticed at least ten other girls as she went. Why couldn't Alison have gotten one of them to help her?

"I figured it would get more light over here, but Doby insists on jumping inside the pot and doing unspeakable things in it. He never did that when I had it back in the corner. Will you just grab ahold and shove?" Alison got down on her knees for leverage and began to pull as Dana maneuvered the giant pot from the other side.

"Whew! Thanks," Alison gasped as they finally wrestled it into its old place. She got to her feet and stared down at the palm. "Now grow, would you?" she growled.

"Is that it, Alison?" Dana asked, anxious to be gone.

"No, actually. Now that I've got you in here, I'd really like you to stay awhile." The housemother smiled, offering Dana the big, comfortable chair, and she knew instantly that the plant had just been a ruse. Alison figured she wouldn't have come in unless it was something innocuous.

"I really . . .well, what is it?" Dana asked hesitantly.

"I've been acting like a real idiot," Alison said. "And I want to apologize."

"Oh? For what?" *For being older than me, for being the person Michael really wants? How can you say you're sorry for that?*

"I didn't see, or didn't want to see, that you

needed somebody. And I wasn't there for you. Last Sunday, when I didn't invite you in, I felt at such a loss. For the first time since I became a housemother, Dana, I was stumped. And that made me angry. The way you looked at me — as though I'd betrayed you — it ate me up inside."

Dana looked at her shoes. "I thought you had, in a way."

"You know, it's not one or the other of us. He can like two people — or five people."

"But not in the same way," Dana blurted out. "It's like my father marrying Eve. He can tell me he still likes my mother until he's blue in the face, but I know he doesn't. He married *Eve*," she repeated with a sob in her throat.

"Hey." Alison sat on the floor, a look of disbelief on her face. "Aren't you getting a little worked up here for nothing? We're not talking marriage, Dana. There are all different ways of caring about people, loving people, even. They don't all end up at the altar." Alison had a small, indulgent smile on her face.

"Sure. But there's the way you love a kid, like me, and then there's the way you feel about an adult. Like you." Dana couldn't help it. She was challenging Alison to say the right thing.

"Maybe. But the love for a kid — as you call yourself — can be satisfying, too."

Dana thought about that one and shook her head.

"Another thing — you don't really think your father's feelings toward you and your sister have diminished one iota because of his new wife and that baby they're going to have, do you?"

"Who told you?" Dana demanded. But she knew.

"Faith and Shelley mentioned it." Alison saw the suspicious look on Dana's face. "I'm telling you the truth. Michael and I don't talk about you."

At the sound of his name, Dana let out a deep sigh. This was what she had feared, exactly. When you kept it inside, you could believe it was just a trick of the light, a fantasy that would eventually go away. But when you said it aloud, it was really there. *Michael and Alison. Alison and Michael. A couple.*

"No, I guess my father still loves me just as much. But he feels different about his wife."

"Of course he does, Dana! That's my point. Every single love is its own thing, unique unto itself and the two people involved. Don't you see the advantage of having the father-daughter variety and also the boyfriend-girlfriend variety you have with Randy, not to mention the roommate variety you have with Faith and Shelley?"

"Yes . . . yes I do." She sat there for a second, gathering momentum. "But I want something big — earthshaking! Randy's just a mild tremor."

Alison tried to hold in her huge guffaw, but couldn't. She laughed until the tears rolled down her face, and finally, Dana saw the humor in it and joined in. When they calmed down, about five minutes later, Alison nodded understandingly. "You'll get your earthquake one day, kid. But if you had them every day, your teeth would fall out."

At last, Dana got up and went over to Alison. She took a breath and leaned down to give her a hug.

"Oh, I'm so glad you did that!" Alison smiled, hugging back. "I hated not talking to you."

"Me, too," Dana admitted. It was like a very large stone had been removed from the bottom of her stomach. "I . . . I guess I shouldn't ask, but will you tell me anyway?" She really needed to know, and Alison saw that she did. "What about you and Michael?"

Alison bit her lip, uncertain of how much to reveal. And the truth was, the question was too hard to answer directly. "Let's put it this way. It's nice. We're happy we met each other. I don't know if it's forever, though."

She hugged Dana again and walked her

to the door of her apartment. "You'll get something good of your own one day, Dana, I promise," Alison said. "And you'll know it's right for you."

As Dana closed the door behind her, she wasn't certain that Alison's prophecy would come true. The only thing she knew definitely was that she had grown up a lot in the past few months. Sometimes, it hurt terribly, but overall, she had to admit, it wasn't half bad.

CHAPTER FOURTEEN

The next three weeks flew by, easy and soaring. Dana's spirits had never been so good, and for some reason, the hard times she'd gone through recently seemed to make the good ones even better. She did brilliantly in her classes, saw Randy every weekend, and was a terrific friend to Faith and Shelley.

"Honestly, Dana," Casey said one Sunday afternoon as they were sitting around Room 407 over a cold plate of eggplant parmigiana that Dana had brought back from Greenleaf. "Maybe we should open a restaurant in Greenleaf the instant we graduate. Who needs college? You can cook, and Faith can do some big photographs of food for decorations, and Shelley can sew the tablecloths."

"Yeah, and what are you going to do for this venture?" Dana asked skeptically.

"Why, my dear, I'm the taster! I'll eat."

And with that, she dug herself out another square and demolished it on the spot.

"Oh, great. With a partner like you, I'd lose money," Dana sighed, removing the pan from her friend's greedy grasp.

"She's right, though, Dana," Shelley agreed. In the past weeks, she'd gained back just the four pounds that made the difference, and she looked terrific. "We should think about that for a summer, maybe. Running a concession in town somewhere."

"And we'll get Pamela to wait tables," Faith said with an evil smirk. "She'll have to do it, or flunk out."

"You know, speaking of Pamela, I think counseling is doing that girl some good," Casey offered, licking her fingers. "I hate to say anything nice about her, but that Michael must have something on the ball."

Dana was silent. There was only one sticking point for her right now, and that was seeing Michael again. Since the day of the horrible blooper, she hadn't been near the library unless it was absolutely essential, and when she did go, she used the back entrance, all the way at the end of the hall and down a flight of stairs from Michael's office. She had managed to avoid him for three whole weeks.

"It's true," Shelley nodded. "Pamela actually said hello to me when we walked into biology lab together. Of course she also wanted me to dissect her frog for her."

"I don't know." Faith shook her head and stretched out flat on the floor, rubbing her full stomach. "I still think she's got a ways to go in the course of basic human conduct."

Dana grinned and started to pick up the remains of their feast.

"Well, back to the salt mines," Casey said, strolling to the window to get the sweater she'd draped over Shelley's piggy bank. "I'll see you guys later. Say, there's Michael. Now, what's he doing here, do you suppose?" She pointed toward the steps of Baker, where the guidance counselor was jogging in place, looking up at their window. He mouthed something to her, which she couldn't hear through the closed windows.

"I think he wants you, Dana," Casey said. "Either that, or he's shooting an ad for jogging clothes on campus."

"Why should he want me?" Dana asked, flustered.

Faith came over and put her hands on Dana's shoulders. "You have to see him sometime, you know. Now's as good a time as any."

Shelley nodded vehemently and gave Dana a little push toward the window. "It's the starting that's important," Shelley reminded her.

Dana walked to the window hesitantly and pushed the casement open a crack.

"What about it, partner?" Michael called

up to her. "I can't make two miles in the cold alone. Come with me?"

Dana looked down at him, and strangely, it was like seeing someone completely new. Why was it, she wondered, that she'd remembered him frozen in time, looking at her the way he had when she'd told him she loved him? Today, he was just Michael, ready for jogging. She wondered, suddenly, if she'd always seen him just the way she wanted him — not the way he really was. She weighed the options and then, realizing that Faith was right, she nodded. "Give me a minute to change," she called back. Then she closed the window. The other three girls were sitting around casually, pretending nothing gigantic was about to happen.

"I'll see you guys later," Dana said, getting into her running gear and starting down the hall.

He was still waiting on the steps, moving around frenetically so as not to freeze up. She smiled at his antics. "You could have come inside," she said.

"What? And break my record for the most stoic man on campus? Not on your life! Well, hurry and warm up — I'm raring to go."

They did some sit-ups and leg stretches, and finally, started off, taking the path they used to take through the maples and out by the town road. It was Sunday-quiet as they crunched the gravel evenly and steadily.

Only the sound of an occasional dog barking as they passed a house broke the mood.

This isn't so bad, Dana thought. *Maybe it was dumb to stay away. Maybe he took what I said with a grain of salt.* Then something else occurred to her. *Maybe girls say that to him all the time. He's young and handsome and, as Faith and Shelley pointed out, a good listener. Who wouldn't fall in love with him? Maybe he gets used to it.* Michael was great, and probably deep down she would always love him, in a way, but she would fall out of love with him because she had to. She knew it.

"You're pretty quiet today," he said finally, when they'd been running for a mile or so.

"Too cold to talk."

"Nah — not for you. You're tough." His breath came in huge white gusts that rose and mingled with the puffy cumulus clouds above them. "Dana," he asked, pounding along, "are we friends?"

"Sure," she nodded, eager to get the subject over with. She really didn't want to discuss anything with him now. The time for that was past.

But Michael stopped in the middle of the road, so she had to stop, too. "Don't you make light of this," he growled at her. "Friendship means a lot to me." He squinted at her, trying to read her expression. "Do you know that I really care about you?"

"Yeah, I know," she muttered. "Now let's go before we freeze."

He put a hand on her arm and looked straight at her with those kind, brown eyes of his. Looking into them, just the way she had when she was falling in love, made her a little sad. He was Alison's, all right, and she was not even in the running. Now, though, she didn't think she wanted to be.

"Maybe," he said, "you'll like me more if you love me less."

The words, painful as they were, made sense. "You may be right," she acknowledged.

"Shall we?" He stretched out his arm, indicating the road ahead, and they plodded off, two people, almost friends again, doing something they both enjoyed. Dana tried to make sense of it all. Of her and Michael, or her and her father, or her and Randy, or her and somebody who might be there on the horizon, someone she hadn't met yet but would, in time. Men! They were harder than any course she would ever take in school. At least you couldn't flunk "Men 1, 2, or 3," she thought with relief. The notion made her laugh.

"You think it's funny," Michael said as they came around, back toward the Canby Hall campus. "This cold weather is killing me."

"It'll be easier in spring," Dana said as they slowed to a walk coming through the gates. "And spring's just around the corner."

He nodded. "That it is. Thanks, Dana." As he jogged off, back toward his house, she wondered what he'd thanked her for.

Faith and Shelley were waiting for her when she got back. The sun had just finished its slow descent and the sky was a wonderful painting in crimson, purple, and gold. The two girls had left the overhead lights off, and they were sitting at the window, staring at the sky. Dana came and joined them.

Her roommates turned to her, looks of concern on their faces. "How'd it go?" Shelley asked, scrutinizing Dana for signs of imminent breakdown.

"It was fine. He was fine. I was fine," Dana said.

"You can tell us the truth, you know," Faith said softly. "We wish you would."

"No, I mean it." Dana shook her head, grasping each girl around the shoulder. "I thought it would be impossible to look at him and talk to him, but there we were, running like we always had. No big deal."

"Whew!" Shelley grinned. "We were so worried about you."

"We thought this might cause a whole other crisis," Faith told her. "So look what we got." She opened Dana's closet and displayed a stack of Kleenex boxes, piled up to the hangers. "We borrowed them from everyone in the dorm, just in case you came back and had a mammoth crying jag."

Dana grinned at the two of them, loving them for their consideration and weirdness. "You two are fantastic — do you know that? You both get the roommate medal of the year."

"Ah, shucks," Shelley shrugged. "What are friends for? You'd do it for either of us," she added, grabbing Dana and hugging her hard. Then Dana reached for Faith and drew her into the circle, and they were smiling.

They sat there in the gathering dark, holding on, and for a while, nothing existed at all except the three of them.

"We're a bunch of mush-heads, you know that?" Faith said at last, breaking the silence.

"So what?" Dana said decisively. She couldn't remember another moment in her life that had meant so much, that had been so perfect. "Let's hear it for friendship," she said softly. Then she hugged her roommates once again, knowing that the bond they had forged over the months they'd been together was growing stronger every day. It would always be theirs, forever.